To the memory of Mary Jane Warner, with thanks, and to my young friend Sage Scofield, who will always belong on Scofield Road—and who knows that I belonged there, too

Contents

A Long Time Ago **Today**

Also by **Sally Warner**

A Long Time Ago **Today**

Sally Warner

Viking

Acknowledgments

I thank my husband, Christopher Davis, both for introducing me to Lake Luzerne (and to Snob Hill) and for sharing its fascinating history with me. I also acknowledge my debt to Nelson Aldrich's *Old Money: The Mythology of America's Upper Class* (New York: Alfred A. Knopf, Inc., 1988) for filling in a few blanks.

VIKING
Published by Penguin Group
Penguin Young Readers Group,
345 Hudson Street, New York, New York 10014, U.S.A.

Published in 2003 by Viking, a division of Penguin Young Readers Group

1 2 3 4 5 6 7 8 9 10

Copyright © Sally Warner, 2003
All rights reserved

LIBRARY OF CONGRESS CATALOGING-IN-PUBLICATION DATA
Warner, Sally.
A long time ago today / by Sally Warner.
p. cm.
Summary: Ever since her mother died six years earlier, twelve-year-old Dilly and her father spend every summer in upstate New York at Mummie's farm, even though Dilly resents how her dead mother continues to intrude on her life.
ISBN 0-670-03604-8 (hardcover)
[1. Death—Fiction. 2. Mothers—Fiction. 3. Friendship—Fiction.
4. New York (State)—Fiction.] I. Title.
PZ7.W24644Lo 2003
[Fic]—dc21   2003005387

Printed in U.S.A.
Set in Rockwell Light

"And then came to her mind those curious questions;
what makes a gentleman? what makes a gentlewoman?"

from *Dr. Thorne*
by Anthony Trollope, 1858

Prologue  **Dilly's Mother**

Like the colors in a flame, a dozen thoughts shimmered in Elspeth Dillon Howell's mind as she lay dying.

Blue: She was only thirty-six.

Red: Peter needed her. Her poor exhausted husband was seated in the sticky vinyl hospital chair beside her hospital bed. His lanky frame—even thinner now than when she'd been admitted to the hospital a week ago—bent forward at the waist like a folding carpenter's ruler. His sleeping face was pressed so hard against the cotton hospital blanket that she knew it would be waffle-marked when he awoke.

That dear face rested only an inch or so from Elle's right arm.

She could feel his breath on her wrist.

Her own arms were placed carefully on the blanket, exactly as if she were already dead, Elle observed, almost interested; they appeared unfamiliar. Well, her arms *were* unfamiliar, Elle thought with some of her old spirit. She managed a frown as she gazed at the weak limbs that had once been parts of a healthy body, tanned, competent, and strong.

Now those same arms were like pale impostors,

pretending still to belong to that body—which had itself come to seem unfamiliar to Elspeth in the last few hours.

Peter's neck would be stiff when he awoke; Elle thought this as if from a distance.

Time or space, she didn't know which word best defined that distance.

Maybe time and space were the same thing.

Indigo: Peter would remarry, she fretted suddenly, feebly, and when he did, their love story would be over forever.

Over.

She frowned harder now, trying to rouse the proper fury at the idea of her husband's imaginary future wife—that witch!—but no such anger even flickered. This unaccustomed lack of passion, of jealousy, almost made Elle smile.

Pink: Peter would marry only if he fell in love again, and if he fell in love it would be because he had known great love— with her, Elspeth. And so even if Peter did marry again, Elle reassured herself, some part of her husband would always remain hers alone. She wanted to reach out and stroke his hair, to comfort him in advance, but she didn't want to wake him.

Also, even such a small effort as lifting a tender finger was seeming increasingly impossible to make.

Elle sighed and turned her head a little to watch for the sun to come up through the curtains she'd insisted be left open all night, so as not to miss this moment. Her thoughts jumped suddenly as they turned to her daughter—her only child.

Lavender-blue: Dilly-dilly.

No, no, Elle pleaded silently. She couldn't die yet! Dilly was only six years old. The little girl wouldn't even be able to picture her mother's face in a year or two, not without looking at a photograph.

Either that, Elspeth thought, clenching her fists, or else every bad moment Dilly had ever shared with her would be remembered, dwelt upon, and magnified. The scoldings, the time-outs, and especially the occasions during the past six months when a reluctant Dilly had either been told to go take a nap or sent into the next room to watch a video, even if it was for the hundredth time, while Mummie took a nap.

Because Mummie wasn't feeling terribly well.

"Under the sea, bum-de-bum-bum, under the sea!" The calypso beat behind those familiar lyrics seemed to float into the room from the not-too-distant past, bringing with them remembered pain—and guilt.

Elle stifled a groan. She thought that she could bear every other good-bye, but not this one. Her little girl still needed her, and so things were not okay.

But at least she'd done what she could for Dilly, Elle tried to reassure herself. Hadn't she finally managed to write that letter—*"future mail,"* the magazine article called it—and then mail it without Peter knowing? Because wasn't he far too distressed already to take on a task that implied all hope was lost?

Slipped into a larger envelope and mailed by a sympathetic nurse, who'd provided the letter's sealing wax—an unnecessarily theatrical touch, in Elle's opinion—the letter had traveled all the way from Pasadena, California, to Lake Luzerne, New York, where Libby had been instructed to tuck it away in a secure location.

Libby was to save the letter for a different, older Dilly.

In spite of Elle's satisfaction at having written that difficult letter, however, her daughter's small, troubled face seemed now to be floating in the still-shadowy trees outside the hospital room.

Green: Dilly's eyes. They were the same changeable sunlit green you saw when lying flat on your back on the lawn at the farm, squinting up through shifting layers of sugar maple leaves.

It was a beautiful way to spend part of a summer afternoon, and a day earlier, Elspeth Howell would have given any amount of money to do it just one more time.

Dilly.

Dilly Howell had short, always-tousled hair of a color that was exactly halfway between its baby blond and the warm brown it would probably become, a straight little nose, and a surprisingly firm—or was that stubborn?—set to her mouth.

Today would probably be their last visit. Elle tried to gather her courage for this encounter, which she guessed would take place just after the nap that always followed her so-called bath. This ritual was an exhausting late-morning affair that took place in bed, involved a nurse's aide, several towels, and two or three washcloths, and left Elspeth shattered with fatigue.

Still, Elle told herself, she had always had a daily bath, and she had no intention of stopping now—simply because she was dying. A Dillon wouldn't let such a little thing stand in the way of her routine. "The very idea," Elle murmured, almost smiling.

After her nap, Peter would lead Dilly into the room, sounding artificially cheerful as he did so. The radio he'd brought a few days ago would be softly playing, as if that might convince Dilly that this was an ordinary morning, the usual visit. It would be almost as if they were at home.

Oh, yes.

Dead flowers would have been plucked from the arrangements that seemed to have been multiplying on their own during the past few days. Brown or broken leaves would have been clipped from houseplants by anxious hospital workers, who hated any farewell scene involving children. The books and magazines Elle no longer had the energy or desire to look at would be stacked high with unnatural precision.

Poor little Dilly, only six years old—and obviously just barely managing to hold it together, no thanks to the grownups around her—was doomed to remember this terrible morning forever, her mother knew.

The music, the flowers, and shiny magazine covers filled with grinning faces.

Dilly was being well cared for, of course—even beautifully cared for, as Elle's family used to put it in the old days. A competent housekeeper was already in place at the Howells' house, as was a young, energetic afternoon baby-sitter, and all of Elle's heartbroken California friends with children Dilly's age were helping to keep the little girl occupied.

But if Dilly's eyes filled with tears during this last visit, her mother thought suddenly, if her small chin wobbled even once, then her own heart would break at last, and it would be over. Finally.

Such a display of emotion on Dilly's part was unlikely, however; the little girl had been growing more and more remote as each day passed. It was almost as though the child were silently storing up complaints. But maybe Dilly was merely coping with an unbearable situation in the only way she knew, Elle told herself.

Certainly Peter was in no condition to notice even dramatic shifts in his little girl's mood.

Maybe her daughter's stoical reaction was a good thing, Elle tried to convince herself. Perhaps that very remoteness was what would help Dilly survive the loss that was going to be hers.

But along with that devastating loss, Elle reassured herself, she was also leaving her daughter something wonderful: the old Dillon property in the Adirondacks that they all called "the farm." This was to go directly to Dilly, at Peter Howell's suggestion.

And so these two things were to be Dilly's legacy: loss, and a place to love.

Elle watched the sky brighten with that weird pale light that comes up behind the San Gabriels just before dawn. Peter sighed in his sleep, and Elle pitied him, though from even farther away than before.

She tried to think of something else, something happier.

Orange: Libby Thorne, her best friend since childhood. Calm, almost serene—Libby was civil, like an orange, Elspeth thought, smiling as she quoted Shakespeare's strange line to herself. Was it from *Much Ado About Nothing?* She had played sassy Beatrice to Libby's Benedick, when they read the play aloud at school in Boston together.

"It's a play on words," she could almost hear their old drama teacher Mrs. Featherton say in her high, hooting way. *"Civil, Seville. Don't you see? All of the oranges came from Seville in those days. You know, girls—in Spain."* This last was added impatiently.

Ho-hum, the girls had mimed behind their teacher's ample back. Still, Elle remembered her words.

But it didn't matter where the words had come from, she thought now; they were just right. Libby was as sweet, nourishing, and refreshing as an orange—even if their relationship had had the bite of a lemon at times.

But that was all in the past. Wasn't it?

Elle wished that Libby could have made it in time to visit;

to talk to her in that special way only a girlfriend could; to stroke damp hair from her temples as if she were a mother, not a best friend.

A mother.

For the first time that morning, Elle almost cried, missing her own mother. *"The impossible Sybil,"* people had called her. But then, Elle's family had been a little impossible, hadn't it? And proudly so. Think of Granny Tat! Libby always said that Granny Tat should have been born a queen—at the very least.

Libby. Libby had said that she couldn't get away until next week.

She would be just in time for the funeral.

The colors Elspeth had been watching began to move, to swirl like a wonderful kaleidoscope. It was an effort for Elle to keep her eyes open as she watched these new patterns, but she knew she had to try to stay awake and alert for a few more hours, at least—long enough to see Dilly one last time and to tell Peter how much she loved him. After that, the nurse had told her, she would probably drift into a coma, which would last—how long?

To her surprise, Dilly's mother discovered suddenly that she didn't care. She knew it was time to close her eyes.

Daylily gold.
White.

Chapter One  **Six Years Later**

Six years later, a furious Dilly Howell jammed some rolled-up underpants into the corner of her duffel bag and bit her lower lip to keep from saying something really nasty to her dad—who was, she admitted to herself, merely trying to make the best of what had become an unavoidable part of every year.

"Come on, sourpuss, it'll be fun. We'll kick back," Peter Howell said, looking oversized as he sat on the frail wicker chair in Dilly's bedroom. He was trying to sound upbeat and modern, but his sad eyes told another story: Peter Howell was still living in the past. Unaware of this, he stretched out his long, khaki-clad legs and crossed them at the ankles, as if demonstrating to Dilly exactly how relaxing six weeks at the farm was going to be.

The farm. Why, Dilly fumed, did everyone insist on still calling it that? The last cows that had grazed its stony fields were herded in by Libby Thorne's grandfather some fifty years ago. He had been encouraged by Granny Tat—her mother's grandmother—to keep them there for the summer simply for the look of the animals, though they also helped to keep the brush down.

Granny Tat had been big on how things looked.

Dilly could almost hear her father's enthusiastic annual refrain: *"Imagine that fresh mountain air! And just think of sitting on the porch, watching the sun go down behind the big field. . . ."*

Sunsets. Exactly what a twelve-year-old girl loved best, Dilly thought sarcastically.

No, she wanted to stay in California, where there were friends to hang out with and a zillion things to do, whenever you wanted to do them.

At Lake Luzerne, the nearest serious mall was more than an hour away, in Albany. She and her dad never even bothered going there.

The nearest movie theater was half an hour away, in Glens Falls. And Dilly had always already seen whatever was playing.

Sasha Thorne, who like Dilly was almost thirteen, and who was Dilly's nearest friend at the farm—really, the only friend Dilly had in the entire state of New York—often stayed just down the road at Libby Thorne's house, which had always been pretty cool. But last year, Sasha had only been there if her Aunt Libby had managed to drag her kicking and screaming, as she put it, from Brooklyn Heights, just across the Brooklyn Bridge from the lower tip of Manhattan. And the city was almost five hours away by car, so Dilly spent many long summer days entirely on her own.

Sasha used to love her Lake Luzerne summers, as had Dilly. After an awkward introduction to each other at age eight, during which Sasha asked Dilly with a sneer where her surfboard was, if she really was from Southern California, and Dilly asked Sasha how many times she had been mugged, if she really lived in Brooklyn, they had—surprisingly!—hit it off.

Surprisingly, because it was hard making friends with someone when grown-ups wanted you to too much, in Dilly's opinion. Especially when that one person was your only hope for having a New York friend at all.

The girls had discovered a mutual love of the woods, though, and they spent hours tramping along the logging paths that crisscrossed the forest at the top of the hill behind Dilly's house, or following the much narrower deer paths they discovered.

Dilly's house, Dilly's fields, Dilly's forest, Dilly's hill. Eighty-nine acres, all hers.

Supposedly.

It was kind of weird, having inherited the farm when she was only six years old. It had been her dad's idea to have the property go directly to her, Dilly had learned—something to do with saving money on estate taxes, or some such thing. "Mummie agreed that this was the way to do it. And Granny Tat would have approved," Peter Howell occasionally told his daughter, as if Granny Tat's would have been the final word.

Sasha must think it was strange that another kid could own so much, Dilly sometimes thought. But maybe Sasha didn't think it strange, because she, Dilly, could never feel conceited about owning that amount of property; her father had drilled her too thoroughly in the farm's long history for any such snootiness.

"This place didn't even belong to your family until 1889, when old Ira Dillon bought it," he told his daughter. "Before that, it was all Thorne property, after it was taken away from that Tory. And the Tory had taken it away from the Indians. Abenaki, I think. But it was given to Benjamin Thorne right after the Revolutionary War, so the Thorne family owned the property for over a hundred years. The place was much larger then, of course—stretched clear down to the river."

But folks call it Snob Hill because of the hundred years *we've* owned the place, Dilly could have added sarcastically, although she never did.

It wasn't something she was proud of.

Sasha had gleefully filled her in on that particular nickname. "First it was 'Thorne Hill,' then 'the old Dillon place,' and then, thanks to your famous Granny Tat, 'Snob Hill.' Congratulations, Dilly! You're the new queen of the snobs," she'd said, cackling her glee.

Instead of passing on this choice tidbit of information to her dad, however, Dilly usually smiled at this point in his story and chimed in with the rest of the tale: "And old Benjamin Thorne is buried down by the river, in the old cemetery." Not too far from Mummie, she could have added.

But then, her father knew that.

The river was what Dilly and Sasha loved best. Less than a mile from the farm, the Hudson River coiled through the Adirondack foothills toward the little town of Lake Luzerne. Narrow this far north, and running clear and clean, the river drew Dilly and Sasha to its side.

Sasha claimed she liked the river so much only because it led back down to her beloved city. But Dilly loved the river because it was beautiful, and because it couldn't belong to *anyone*—and so there was no burden attached to it.

The girls would coast down the hill to the river on whatever battered second- or third-hand bikes they'd scrounged for the summer, tug their mesh rubber-bottomed river shoes onto sweaty feet, and balance like seagulls on the round stones that were exposed when the river was low. Two years ago, when they were ten, the river was unusually high; Dilly and Sasha had a rock-skipping contest that year that had lasted two hours. It was a marathon, practically, and the loser—Dilly—had had to give Sasha a half-hour back rub.

"This is exactly like being at a spa," Sasha murmured, almost purring. "A little to the left, please. *Ouch!*"

Every year, no matter what shape the river was in, what the girls liked best was to find a deserted bank, preferably one matted with the wild thyme that grew so freely in the area, check the ground for bugs at city-dwelling Sasha's insistence, clear away any twiggy rubble, and then sit down and talk.

And talk.

In the last couple of years, however, Sasha had become so involved with her city life that spending weeks away from Brooklyn Heights seemed to her like a crazy thing to do—and she said so frequently, to Dilly's dismay.

Dilly had less of a choice about coming to Lake Luzerne. Her mother used to spend entire summers there when she was growing up, having lived in Boston, only a long day's drive away. "I suppose you and Dilly will want to spend your vacations at the farm," she had told her husband at the hospital one afternoon. "That'll be nice." Her speech had sounded a little blurred.

Although these words were spoken casually, however, as were many other of her drowsy observations made during her heavily medicated last few weeks, they—along with the other observations—quickly assumed the authority of commandments after her death.

Peter Howell built a sort of scaffolding of what he thought were his dead wife's wishes; it was as if he hoped that imaginary structure might be able to hold Dilly—and himself, for that matter—above the black water that seemed to flow so swiftly beneath them.

At first, that scaffold was something to cling to, and if over the years it had become more like a prison, Peter Howell appeared not to notice. Elle's word had become law, and neither Dilly nor her father realized just how accidentally that had happened.

But the yearly trek east made things difficult for Dilly at home in Pasadena. It was hard enough for a girl nowadays to make really good friends and keep them, Dilly mused bitterly, without then packing up and leaving town for six whole weeks. And on her birthday, too! How cheesy was that, to get to go to everyone else's parties all year long but never invite them to yours? *"Sor-ry!"*

A kid could end up friendless that way.

Not that Becka and Fran—Dilly's two closest California friends—ever actually complained. But that was the thing: they weren't really close enough to her to care, in Dilly's opinion. Not say-anything, blurt-it-all-out, get-past-the-surface close.

Not *Sasha* close.

But maybe Becka and Fran *would* be deep-down friends like that, Dilly thought, if they just had the chance to hang out together during the summer—when things had a chance to get real.

And so going back to the farm each summer was not only a waste of a perfectly good summer, if you asked Dilly, it was downright risky. Her California friendships, fragile as they were, could shift and change. She might return home to— who knew what?

Just because her mother had left her the old place in her will, that didn't mean Dilly and her dad had to fly east like demented migrating birds for the rest of their lives, did it?

Who did her mom think she *was*, bossing them around that way?

But if he, Peter Howell, could use up the bulk of his vacation time this way each year, her dad seemed silently to argue early each summer, why couldn't stubborn, ungrateful Dilly at least pretend to cooperate?

Her dad simply did not have a clue as to how things changed once you started growing up.

Catching a glimpse of herself in the mirror, Dilly straightened her shoulders. Almost five feet six inches tall now, although she was not yet thirteen, Dilly was still trying to get used to her new height. Her skin was lightly tanned after three weeks of summer vacation, and her short brown hair glinted with sunny highlights.

She looked okay, Dilly admitted to herself.

She wished that her father would just leave her alone, however. How was she supposed to pack her three new bras with him watching like the legal eagle he was? Wasn't there such a thing as privacy around here?

Her new bras! That was one of the good things about not having a mom, Dilly reminded herself. You could pick out really cool underwear, if your dad gave you enough money. And money didn't seem to be a problem for Peter Howell. His work as an estate lawyer took care of that, and there were never any trials, so his partner was easily able to take up the slack, as her dad put it, during the detested trips east each summer.

Dilly almost laughed in triumph, thinking of the colorful lace-trimmed bits of satin that nestled like a stack of sleeping butterflies in her lingerie drawer. Turquoise, fire-engine red, and lavender blue: Those bras were *hot!* Her poor friends were having to make do with pathetic, unadorned little triangles held together by strips of white elastic that looked like bandages.

Ugh.

There were lots of good things about not having a mother, Dilly told herself—or any brothers or sisters either, for that matter. Basically, you got to have everything your own way.

Well, almost everything.

"Just think how great it will be, sitting on the porch and watching the sunset," her father was saying. "Won't that be fun?"

It sounded as though he were asking a question. But he wasn't.

Dilly sighed and started rolling up some T-shirts for the duffel bag.

She'd better pretend, at least, to go along with her dad's fake enthusiasm—before he trotted out the magic words: *"Please, Dilly. Do it for Mummie."*

Because Dilly didn't think she could bear hearing those words one more time.

Chapter Two 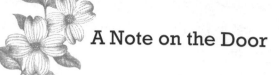 A Note on the Door

As if the date were carved in stone, Dilly and her father flew to Albany each year on July seventh. By leaving then, they could attend the annual Fourth of July picnic with their neighbors at home in Pasadena and still have a couple of days to pack.

They returned to Pasadena on August twentieth, two days after Dilly's birthday, which by tradition had always been celebrated at the farm. The day after her birthday, Dilly and Peter Howell always paid a solemn visit to the old cemetery down by the river—to say good-bye both to Elspeth Howell and to the farm for another year.

A town in the southernmost foothills of the New York's Adirondacks State Park, Lake Luzerne was about an hour's drive north of Albany. The mountainous area teemed with insect life—mosquitos, gnats, no-see-ums—from spring into early summer, but after July fourth, local tradition had it, most of the region's pesky insect life fled for parts unknown.

Hah! There were lots of stories like that about the place that weren't true, in Dilly's opinion. For example, how "comfortable" the old place was. When she tried to point out to her father that they were leaving an up-to-date air-conditioned house and a swimming pool in Pasadena each summer for weeks spent in a rambling two-hundred-year-old structure in New York where things routinely broke down for no apparent reason, and where they didn't even have an electric fan, her dad always said, "But we're lucky at the farm, Dilly. It's the coolest spot for miles around, up there on the hill. You don't even *need* a fan! Mummie and Granny Tat were always so proud of that."

Which pretty effectively squelched Dilly's campaign to buy an electric fan for her bedroom, even though "darling Mummie," as Dilly privately—and bitterly—called her, was no longer the one lying panting for a breeze on impossibly twisted sheets each summer, swatting at mosquitos that whined past her ears in the dark like tiny Stealth bombers.

No bugs, and always the perfect temperature. What a joke!

The Howells' travel arrangements were made by Mr. Howell's secretary, who clasped Dilly in an emotional cushiony hug every time the girl set foot in her father's Los Angeles office. "Poor little thing," she sometimes whispered, even now, six years after Elspeth Howell had died.

There were no direct flights between Los Angeles and Albany, New York, the nearest large airport to the farm, so it was necessary for Dilly and her father to change planes in Chicago. But Dilly liked Chicago; the airport, anyway. She sometimes pretended she lived in that city and was striding through O'Hare's wide glossy corridors merely to collect her suitcase and head home from vacation—preferably in Hawaii, though she'd never been there—rather than simply to change gates.

Instead, of lingering in Chicago, though, she and her father settled wearily into their new seats on what was always a dinkier plane than the one that had left Los Angeles. "What do you think it's going to be?" Dilly's dad invariably asked, nudging her with his elbow. "Those weird dusty peanuts, or the pack of stale miniature pretzels you can never tear open?"

And Dilly always tried to smile.

She did it this year, too.

It was humid in Albany when they finally landed late on Sunday afternoon. This stifling heat surprised Dilly anew each summer, and she felt dumb for not remembering the creepy dampness that seemed to make even breathing difficult, much less hauling duffel bags through a steaming airport parking lot. "Why couldn't we have rented one of those little carts?" Dilly asked, trying not to whine.

Peter Howell paused and patted with his handkerchief at the trickle of perspiration that was making its way down his cheek. "Your mother used to say that baggage carts were for weaklings. She said if people knew how to pack properly, they wouldn't need carts," he told his daughter, as if reciting something he'd memorized.

But her mother had always kept a complete wardrobe at the farm, Dilly argued silently, so really, what had she needed to pack? And the Albany airport was probably a lot bigger now than it had been when Elspeth Howell last landed there. It certainly seemed as if it was much harder to get around at the airport than it once had been.

Her mother had been a snob about the weirdest things. But her mother was dead. Couldn't they vary their routine even a little?

And anyway, maybe she, Dilly, *was* a weakling, a wimp. Perhaps she wasn't a true Dillon, not deep down in her heart. Hadn't anyone ever thought of that? Wasn't she a Howell, too?

But her *dad* didn't even act like a Howell, Dilly answered herself silently. It was as if his wife's family was a giant wave that had buried whatever lay in its path. Quoting his dead wife and her grandmother at the drop of a hat, and obediently trotting off to New York each year the way he did—what kind of a wimp did that make him?

Dilly blushed just asking herself this disloyal question. After all, didn't they have fun together in California? Desert camping trips each spring in Anza-Borrego, and winter skiing at Mammoth. He skied down slopes she would never dare to try.

"Look for the little red flag," her father instructed her, and

Dilly stopped staggering and carrying on one-sided arguments long enough to scan the cars' antennae that bristled across the seemingly infinite expanse of the airport's new long-term parking lot.

The Howells had had a standing business arrangement with the Lake Luzerne garage: the mechanic and his wife would caravan the Howells' old Chevy Lumina down to the airport parking lot and leave it there, tattered red flag flying, for Peter Howell to pick up each July seventh.

This procedure would be reversed every August twentieth, when the Lumina would be returned to Lake Luzerne to spend the winter up on blocks in one of the Howells' old barns, surrounded by old sleds, cracked saddles, shrouded porch furniture, hundred-year-old farm equipment, paint cans, and lawn mowers.

"There it is," her dad called out, pointing his finger diagonally across a few lines of shimmering cars. "Hang in there, Dilly-dill. We'll be on the Northway before you know it."

"Great," Dilly mumbled, and she prepared for the final push to reach the car. An hour's drive—with the air conditioner off, naturally! because what were they, weaklings?—awaited them.

No, wait—the air conditioner didn't even work anymore. But at least they could roll down the car windows. And the air *was* pretty nice up here, Dilly admitted silently. Or it would be, once they got on the road.

❖ ❖ ❖

It wasn't only the mechanic and his wife whom they relied upon, Dilly thought, watching soothing waves of rounded trees roll by, trees that were so different from the dusty yellow-greens of the palms that spiked Dilly's California neighborhood like random exclamation marks. No, she thought—it took a whole team of Lake Luzerne people to make the Howells' summer stays possible.

For example, an uncle of Libby's who lived down on Stony Bend Lane mowed the Howells' fields—the big one and the two little ones—with his tractor a few times each year. He was retired from his job at the paper mill in Corinth, but he had land of his own to care for. He liked Peter Howell, though, and didn't mind helping out.

Another of Libby's relatives was a plumber down in Corinth, and he was in charge of closing the farm for the winter, a painstaking process that involved flushing every last bit of water from the pipes. If that wasn't done correctly, generations of Dillons had learned the hard way, expanding ice made the pipes split, and then when the water was turned back on in the spring, the ensuing rush of water could ruin walls and even bring down ceilings.

Marti Oller, an energetic volunteer at the Lake Luzerne Library where Libby Thorne was head librarian, stocked the refrigerator and pantry for the Howells. She also got everything shiny clean in welcome for the Howells' arrival each summer and scrubbed the old place down when they left. While they were there, she came in to clean once a week and helped out with the extra work entailed when house guests came to stay for a night or two.

Some days, Mrs. Oller was the only person with whom Dilly spoke, other than her father. It was nice talking to a person who had actually known her mom, Dilly admitted to herself.

Elspeth's old friend Libby Thorne took care of everything else: making sure the P.O. forwarded the Howells' mail after they'd left each August; collecting the *Post Stars* that sometimes continued to pile up after their departure; walking through the freezing house from time to time to make sure things were okay. It was as though she were a nurse taking the pulse of the old place when no one was in residence.

Apart from Libby, who always said that what she did was nothing, since she was only being neighborly, all of these people were paid. Dilly knew Lake Luzerne inside out, however, so she realized that there was no *way* anyone would lift a finger to help—no matter how broke they were—if they didn't happen to feel like it, if they didn't like you at least a little bit.

But if any of these arrangements ever fell through—with the mechanic and his wife, with Libby and her relatives, with Marti Oller—then chaos would ensue, Dilly knew, and the yearly visit would be in jeopardy.

Boo-hoo.

"Dilly, wake up—we're almost there," Peter Howell said, turning right from 9N onto the narrow lane that was Riverview Road.

"What time is it?" Dilly said, yawning.

"It's six forty-five P.M.," her father told her, precise as usual. "Look sharp! Maybe we'll see a deer."

Dilly tried to stretch in her seat, and she took a swig from the nearly warm water bottle that nestled in the car's drink holder. She did want to be alert—not so much for deer spotting as for a more secret pleasure: the dreamlike experience of seeing a familiar place after ten months' absence.

Hadn't there been a whiskery gray horse in that little pasture? Weren't the daylilies blooming by this time last year? What had happened to that V-shaped tree that used to grow near that old stone fence?

"Libby painted her porch," Dilly's father reported, slowing down as they passed the one place visible from their own house. "It'll be good seeing her again," he added, seemingly to himself. He blushed a little and patted the steering wheel, as if in time to some music that Dilly couldn't hear.

Dilly stirred uneasily in her seat. "We'll probably be pretty busy doing our own stuff," she reminded her dad. "And Libby is still running the library, don't forget. The house does look good, though," she conceded, seeing the sudden frown on her father's face. She glared back over her shoulder at Libby's house and remembered the story: In 1951, eight years after her husband's death, Granny Tat—the elegant Tatiana Prescott Dillon, Dilly's great-grandmother—had had what was now Libby's house constructed, to be sold to an old college roommate who'd been recently widowed.

And why had Granny Tat wanted the little house built and then sold to a friend for very little money? Not to earn some extra cash, certainly—but so that she could see a pretty light twinkling down the lane when she looked out the window at night, according to family lore. Also, she wanted to have someone familiar to talk to when she felt like it.

That last part of the story had always bothered Dilly; typical Snob Hill, she told herself. It served her great-grandmother right when the widow fell in love, remarried, and moved away, selling the place to Libby Thorne's father.

Granny Tat wasn't perturbed by this, though, not that Dilly had heard, when being told the old family stories. But then, she couldn't ever remember her seeming ruffled about anything at all. Of course, she'd died when Dilly was only four. But Granny Tat had always liked the Thorne family, so apparently they passed muster as new neighbors.

"And here we are," Dilly's father said, swinging into the gravel-strewn driveway. "Oh no, give me strength," he added, suddenly gloomy. "There's a note on the door."

A note on the door.

That was always bad news when you were arriving at the farm.

What would it be this time? A cracked water pipe? A room that suddenly and mysteriously couldn't be heated? Or would it be mice-in-the-pantry-chipmunks-in-the-rafters-broken-refrigerator-backed-up-septic-tank-well-run-dry?

Who knew?

Dilly's heart fluttered a little: Maybe they would have to turn around and drive back to the airport!

"Might as well get this over with," Dilly's dad called over his shoulder, taking the wide stone stairs that lead up to the porch two at a time. He snatched the note from where it had been tacked to the wood frame of the screen door as Dilly struggled to free herself from an unfamiliar seat belt.

"What does it say?" she asked.

"I don't know," was her father's astonishing reply. "It's not for me, it's for you."

Chapter Three  Dear Mummie

The note *couldn't* be for her. Sasha was in the city, and she always communicated through e-mail—when Dilly was in California, anyway, Sasha being the absolute master of all technology, to hear her tell it. And who else did Dilly know around here? "Are you sure it's for me?" she asked, climbing the stairs to the porch.

But Peter Howell had already handed Dilly the envelope and moved on to his next task, which was finding the correct key to unlock the front door—the kitchen door, really, since that was the only one anyone had used for the last fifty years.

"Eureka," Dilly's father said, turning the key and then throwing his right hip against the paint-layered door, which swung open with a squeak. A suddenly familiar smell floated out to Dilly: a blend of furniture polish, soap, and lavender, with a musty undertone—long-stored potatoes, perhaps— that never quite disappeared, no matter how hard Mrs. Oller scrubbed.

Dilly stared at the pale blue envelope with the thumbtack hole at the top. Whose handwriting was this?

"Just open it, why don't you?" her father asked, having

made a quick, investigatory loop around the first floor, probably to reassure himself that everything really was okay.
"We'll bring the bags in later, but we've earned a little sup-
per first. I'll see what Marti left for us," he said, and then he
disappeared into the pantry, a tucked-away room adjoining
the kitchen. This space primarily housed the refrigerator, a
washer and dryer, and a full summer's supply of canned and
dry food.

On another wall, long shelves piled high with stacks of
china were crowded between the fridge and the far wall of
the room. Some of the pieces were so old by now that their
original purpose was forgotten. Were these celery glasses?
Carving knife holders? Asparagus plates or oyster dishes?

Who knew?

The far wall was crammed full of a long line of dusty rain-
coats, slickers, parkas, stiff canvas jackets, and even faded se-
rapes, all hung on hooks. Beneath the coats, a row of creased
riding boots, old rubber rain shoes, and a virtual L. L. Bean
museum of footwear stood perfectly lined up, as if ready to
march forward into the scuffed wall.

No one liked to throw anything away at the farm. *"You
never know when it might come in handy,"* the old saying went.

"Okay, I'll open it," Dilly said faintly, both to herself and to
her father, and she sank down onto the porch's creaky rattan
sofa. Why, she asked herself, did she have such a funny feeling about this note? *Bad* funny.

She eased open the flap, slid out a folded piece of

notepaper, and looked quickly at the signature: It was from Libby Thorne, their neighbor just down the road.

Dilly started to read.

> *Dear Dilly,*
>
> *Welcome back! The old place has certainly missed you. And let me be the first to wish you an early happy birthday, while I'm at it. Thirteen is quite an important age.*
>
> *Which brings me to the real point of this note, Dilly. As you know, your mother and I were good friends. Best friends, really. And I think she would want this summer, this birthday, to be an especially mean- ingful one for you. This is why I have decided that now is the time to give you the letter she wrote to you just before she died.*
>
> *I haven't read it, of course, but I know it is sure to be both loving and inspirational. Your mother had so much that she wanted to share with you, Dilly!*
>
> *I know that Elle would have given anything to be with you this special summer. I am hoping that the let- ter she left will be the next best thing to having her here.*
>
> > *Fondly,*
> > *Libby Thorne*

Peter Howell poked his head out of the kitchen. "We've got cold chicken, potato salad, and sliced tomatoes," he announced happily. "And peach cobbler for dessert."

Heart thudding, Dilly stuffed Libby's note back into its envelope, stood up and put it in her pocket, and went in to the kitchen, letting the screen door speak for her with a noisy slam. "I'll just go wash up," she told her dad, her throat aching with the words.

Dilly was *angry*.

Libby had it all wrong; Dilly was certain of this. *"Loving and inspirational,"* hah! Know-it-all and bossy was probably more like it. After all, practically every little thing she and her dad did—how they spent their summers, even—was already decided by figuring out what Elspeth Dillon Howell would have wanted them to do. Wasn't that bad enough?

And now there was this letter, Dilly fumed. It would probably include a list of such things as what makeup she was to be allowed to wear, and when. Also, what kind of clothes were most suitable for young girls. Maybe her mom's letter would even announce when she could begin dating—and what colleges she should apply to, when the time came.

Just what she needed, advice from her mother. Who wasn't even around anymore!

"Dear Mummie," Dilly muttered savagely as she scrubbed her hands almost raw in the bathroom sink.

> *Dear Mummie,*
>
> *Look, I'm sorry you're dead and everything, okay? That must be really terrible for you. But why can't you just leave us alone?*
>
> *I mean, look at things from my point of view! First*

you go and die on me when I'm just a little kid. But you
don't just actually leave, or anything. Oh no, you have
to stick around and haunt us. "Mummie never liked
paper napkins." "Mummie always thought nail polish
was vulgar on little girls." Look, I don't *want any "inspi-*
ration" from you, okay? Stop bossing us around!

　　　You're dead, don't you get it??? GET OFF MY
BACK!!!!

　　　　　　　　　　　　　　Fondly, your ex-daughter Dilly

"Dilly?" her father asked, rapping softly on the bathroom
door. "Is everything all right in there?"

"I'm okay," she called out, her voice a little wobbly. "You
go sit down, Dad. I'll be with you in a second."

"Well, if you're sure," her father said.

"I'm sure."

Dilly couldn't bring herself to read Libby's note again until
just before bedtime.

Chapter Four   Forget About It!

She stormed down the road to Libby's house early the next morning—before she could lose her nerve. She did *not* want Libby to ruin both her summer and her birthday by delivering that letter from her mother.

And the sooner she told Libby so, the better.

It was going to be another hot day. Bluebirds—performing their insect-gathering acrobatics early, in an effort to save energy—darted from the small wooden houses that perched on the fence along the edge of the Howells' biggest field.

Libby hadn't left for the library yet, Dilly was glad to see; her red Honda was still pulled up next to the freshly painted porch. The front door opened just as Dilly raised her hand to knock. "Oh, you're here!" Libby said, sweeping Dilly into a hug. "Sasha will be so glad to see you again. And I'm happy, too."

Reluctant, stiff, Dilly hugged her back. *It's not Libby's fault. It's not Libby's fault,* she repeated silently to herself. Granny Tat's handed-down advice, *"Never quarrel with your neighbors—especially in the country!"* also reverberated somewhere in Dilly's mind.

"Let me get a good look at you," Libby said, holding Dilly at arms' length.

She didn't hurry as she looked, and Dilly took her own time staring back at Libby Thorne. She must be in her early forties; her hair was now faded brown in color. It had been white-blond when she was a child, worn then in long pale braids that Dilly remembered from the many snapshots of her own mother's Lake Luzerne summers.

Now, it was styled short in a borderline-spiky cut that looked good on her. Its color reminded Dilly of the soft feathers she sometimes found lying on the path when walking in the woods.

You always kind of worried about what had happened to the bird who'd lost its feathers like that.

Libby's eyes were the same vivid chicory-flower blue they always had been, of course, but tiny lines were now beginning to crease their outer corners, and there were new shadows under those eyes.

She looked as though she'd been worrying about something; losing sleep, anyway.

Libby had been married once, Dilly remembered hearing—but only briefly, and that had been a long time ago. Her husband had been a college friend of her brother's, Dilly had been told, probably by Sasha. The young couple had lived in New York City.

Maybe Libby hadn't liked it there.

Sasha mentioned once that Libby sometimes dated a French Canadian businessman in Montreal, a man Sasha had sarcastically nicknamed "Jean-Paul Hottie." Sasha had been introduced to him once and claimed he was the most boring man she had ever met in her entire life, or any of her previous lives. But the relationship didn't seem to be going anywhere, Sasha had reported last summer. She'd sounded relieved.

"You're beautiful, Dilly," Libby told her, and she tugged her inside the front door. "You look more and more like Elspeth every year."

The two women had been best friends, Dilly reminded herself—friends since childhood, in fact. And that was why Libby had been entrusted with that blasted letter.

"I don't really look like her," Dilly said, trying to keep her voice steady. "Mummie had dark brown eyes, not green ones like mine. And she was really delicate and short. And prettier, too," she added, mumbling so that Libby wouldn't think she was fishing for more compliments.

Because she wasn't fishing, she meant it. Wasn't her dad always going on about how beautiful her mother had been? And who could live up to that?

Still smiling, Libby shook her head, obviously uncon-vinced. "Listen, can I fix you some eggs?" she asked, gestur-ing toward the kitchen. "I have to leave for the library pretty soon, but everything's still out on the counter. It'll be easy—no trouble at all."

"No thanks," Dilly said, pulling away a little. "I just wanted to talk to you. You know, about—about—"

"About the letter?" Libby asked, finishing Dilly's sentence for her. She looked happy and excited, as though imagining how thrilled Dilly must be feeling.

Dilly nodded, still angry but suddenly mute.

"Come on, sit down," Libby said, suddenly concerned, and she led Dilly over to a deep-cushioned navy blue sofa. Dilly sank down into it as if her legs could no longer support her. "Are you okay, Dilly? What's wrong?"

Dilly gulped some air. "Is it true?" she finally asked, eyes wide. "Did my mother really write me a letter? *Six years ago?*"

Libby nodded, but she looked a little confused. "Well, yes," she said slowly. "But didn't you—"

"She wrote it to me when she knew she was dying?" Dilly persisted, interrupting. She was still trying to wrap her mind around this weird idea.

Libby nodded again, looking even less sure of herself this time. "She wanted it to be a surprise," she told Dilly.

Dilly struggled to her feet, clutching a throw pillow to her chest as if for protection. "Oh, it's a surprise all right," she said, scowling. She began to pace back and forth along the length of Libby's small living room.

Alarmed now, Libby stood up too. "Dilly, I don't under-stand. This was supposed to be a nice thing, honey."

"Well, it's *not* nice," Dilly said. "It's creepy! Who did she think she was?"

"She was your mother, Dilly," Libby said, her voice cooler now. "And she obviously didn't write that letter to upset you. She thought it would make you happy."

"She doesn't even know me," Dilly cried out. "Not anymore."

"Okay," Libby said. "So she doesn't know you. Forget about the letter, then—just don't open it."

"Well, don't give it to me!" Dilly shot back.

"Don't *give* it to—Dilly, are you saying you didn't open the letter yet?" Libby asked, looking both baffled and angry, Dilly was surprised to see.

"How could I have opened it when you still have it?" she asked. "Just rip it up, Libby—that's all I'm saying. And don't go telling my dad about it, either."

"Rip it *up*?" Libby asked, sounding flabbergasted, now. "A last letter from your *mother*? I obviously made a mistake even telling you about it. If you're not ready to read it yet, Dilly, I'd better just go get it. I'll hang onto it for a while."

"Aha! *'Go get it.'* It's here, isn't it?" Dilly asked, looking wildly around the tidy little room. "Where is it?" she asked, whirling around to glare accusingly at various pieces of furniture. Was the letter in that little curly-maple desk? Tucked between two books in the built-in bookshelf under the stairs? Lying on the kitchen counter?

Libby shook her head. "Where the letter is doesn't really matter, Dilly. Not if you don't want to read it."

"It matters to me. *It's mine.*"

"Not if you haven't opened it yet," Libby said crisply, brushing an invisible speck of lint from her khaki slacks. "I was trying to follow your mother's instructions, but now obviously is not the right time for you to have that letter."

"It will never be the right time," Dilly said scornfully. "It was a horrible, selfish thing for her to do!"

"Okay, it'll never be the right time," Libby echoed, holding up her hands in mock surrender. "I can live with that. So just forget about it. Forget this whole thing ever happened."

"But I *can't* forget about it! That's like telling me there's a poisonous snake hidden somewhere, and then saying not to worry about it. Tell me, is it here—in this room?"

Libby shook her head. "I'm not saying, so you can just stop asking. But I'll tell you this much. You could search this place from top to bottom and you wouldn't be one step closer to finding Elle's letter."

"That must mean it's at the farm! You hid it somewhere at the farm, didn't you?"

"I didn't hide it anywhere," Libby said. "And what would you do if you found the letter, Dilly? Tear it up, like you told *me* to do?"

Dilly didn't answer, but she could picture herself doing exactly that: ripping the letter to shreds, unopened. That would teach her mom a lesson about trying to boss her around from beyond the grave!

It would probably be a thick envelope, Dilly thought, almost feeling the heavy paper beneath her tingling fingertips. And it would say *Dilly* on the front, or maybe *Dillon Halliburton Howell,* the ridiculous name her parents had saddled her with—a name that made her sound more like a law firm than an ordinary kid.

But would she even recognize her mother's handwriting? The thought that she might not made Dilly feel sick to her stomach.

"I have to leave for work, Dilly," Libby was saying. She sounded exhausted.

Dilly stared at her, almost hating the woman, her mother's best friend. And all at once, it was as though the anger Dilly felt toward her long-dead mother was boiling over—onto Libby Thorne. "You're really not going to tell me where that letter is, are you?" Dilly said to her neighbor.

Libby looked at Dilly for a few seconds without speaking. Then she said, "I think maybe I should speak to your father about this, honey. I'm really sorry I've disturbed you so deeply. I had no idea that—"

"That *what*?" Dilly interrupted, furious. "That I'd expect you to give me something that already belongs to me? And don't you dare go tattling to my dad about this! It'll just make him sad. Unless—is that what you wanted in the first place?

An excuse to start hanging around my father, having cozy
little heart-to-heart talks and everything? *How pathetic!*"

Even as she said these ugly words, Dilly knew she had
gone too far. She had quarreled with her neighbor, violating
one of Granny Tat's commandments. She had also implied
that Libby was secretly in love with her dad. And calling her
mom's best friend "pathetic" would have hurt the woman's
feelings, maybe even her pride—which was worse, at least
in this part of the Adirondacks.

Libby might never forgive her. Feuds had lasted generations around here for less.

Dilly wanted to take back what she had said, or at least
some of it. So her dad had blushed when they'd first driven
by Libby's house. So he'd said it would be good seeing Libby
again. So what? That didn't mean he wanted to marry her!

And Libby didn't even know what Peter Howell had said.
It wasn't exactly fair to treat her as if she were some man-
hungry vampire.

I'm sorry, I'm sorry, I'm sorry, Dilly thought fiercely, as if
hoping that Libby could somehow pick up on this apology
vibe. She would have to, if they were to patch things up—
because Dilly was completely unable to speak.

Libby didn't appear to have heard Dilly's silent apology,
though. For Libby, some invisible line seemed to have been
crossed. She looked both angry and stunned. "I think you'd
better just leave, Dillon," she said.

And so Dilly left.

Chapter Five

As she ran down the road toward home, tears blurred Dilly's vision. A small plaid figure at the far end of the field—her father—lifted his hand in silent greeting, and Dilly mimed a falsely cheerful response.

She raced through the kitchen without grabbing even so much as a banana, although breakfast was usually her favorite meal.

Not today.

Dilly stomped upstairs, slammed her bedroom door shut with abandon, since there was no one in the house to hear the noise, and flung herself onto her unmade bed. "Ahhh!" she screamed into her pillow, and then she bit down hard, leaving marks on the cross-stitched pillow slip.

How, she wondered, could she be feeling so many different things at the same time? What was wrong with her?

Number one, she was furious with her mother for trying to haunt her with that birthday letter.

Number two, she was totally ashamed of how she'd behaved toward Libby—and of what she'd said to her.

Number three, she was seriously annoyed with Sasha for

not being here at Lake Luzerne to make things better, with her sarcastic take on things. Sasha made the place—the entire *town*—seem bigger, somehow. Sasha owed it to her to be here!

And *number four,* Dilly felt guilty about her father.

But that was just plain dumb, she tried to tell herself. Her dad was fine. So what if he was already off inspecting every square inch of the place, making lists of the chores that needed to be done during his so-called vacation? The fences mended, the saplings sawn down, the outbuildings painted? He liked keeping busy. He liked making lists.

But maybe he would also *like* having a heart-to-heart talk with Libby Thorne, a nagging voice in Dilly's head observed. Maybe he was ready to start dating again. *Openly.*

Because it wasn't as if her dad had become a monk after her mother died, Dilly reminded herself; he had simply confined his social life to lunch dates during working hours, or to the nights when Dilly was staying over at a friend's house.

People were probably always trying to fix him up with someone. Other kids' moms—eager to introduce him to their single friends—were certainly interested in his marital status.

Officially, Dilly couldn't tell them a thing. Her father never talked about anyone special, much less suggested that Dilly actually meet someone he happened to be dating.

Unofficially, however, Dilly had become a pretty good snoop over the years. Fancy restaurant leftovers in the fridge, florist bills left on the hall table, even a long red hair on her dad's jacket—all these things revealed her father's secret life to Dilly.

But it obviously wasn't one that he felt was serious enough—important enough!—to share with Dilly. So she still had her father all to herself.

She got to choose the restaurants, the camping spots, the beaches to go to.

But maybe that would change someday, she thought. And how was she going to feel about that? "Shut up," she shouted out loud, and she sat up in bed.

No, Dilly reassured herself—she didn't have to worry about her dad and Libby. Just as Libby Thorne had never displayed any romantic interest in her father, neither had Dilly's dad ever seemed especially fascinated by Libby. She was just his dead wife's friend. That's why he had said it would be good to see her again.

And they'll never be any closer now, thanks to you, the nagging voice in her head chimed in. "Shut *up*," Dilly yelled once more. "This is all your fault, darling Mummio! You should have stuck around, that's all."

Dilly vowed to find that infuriating letter if it killed her.

The house at Snob Hill had been built in three stages over the course of almost two hundred and fifty years. Originally it had been a simple rectangle with stairs up the middle. The first big addition was made in 1847. This date had been carved proudly at one side of the kitchen door, the elongated 8 and stately, curved 7 revealing their age. Dilly liked to trace the numbers with her finger, imagining the carver: his square brown beard, his straw hat, his suspenders.

After her great-great-grandfather bought the place in 1889, the staircase had been made fancier, Dilly had been told, and the kitchen and bathrooms made more up-to-date. Dillon possessions had started rolling in, too, accumulating gradually over the years.

Unwanted bureaus, desks, and bedsteads were moved in from various elegant Boston residences; jewel-toned rugs, silken wall hangings, and hand-painted porcelain were shipped to Lake Luzerne from energetic family treks to Persia and China; the carefully preserved contents of unused hope chests made their eventual way there, too. All these costly things and exotic fragrances transformed the place from the simple farmhouse it once had been into a place of some elegance.

Dilly, however, longed for modern things: sleek low sofas upholstered in impossibly bright colors; gleaming bare floors; uncurtained windows, empty spaces to clack around in while wearing the highest stiletto heels possible.

And what was the deal with *hope chests*, Dilly asked herself, shaking her head. What a weird concept! If *she* had a hope chest, it would only need to contain one thing: a one-way ticket out of Lake Luzerne.

Many of the house's old linens still lay folded with fading tissue and tucked-in crumbling sprigs of lavender—sent home in boxes from early-twentieth-century Dillon trips to France—in the big painted chest on the upstairs landing. Whenever Dilly had been obliged to open the linen chest when she was little, which rarely happened, as its heavy lid could suddenly snap down with finger-mashing ferocity, she'd imagined that spirits might come pouring out of it—like at the climax of *Raiders of the Lost Ark*, when the bad guys opened the ark and the ghosts roared out. *Whoosh!*

Maybe that chest was where Libby had hidden that stupid letter, Dilly thought, her eyes narrowing. Libby had practically told her the letter was at the farm, hadn't she? *"I'd better just go get it,"* she'd said.

What better place to hide a haunted letter than in a haunted linen chest?

Of course, there were other places at the farm where the letter might be, Dilly admitted to herself—countless places. The playroom, for instance!

The upstairs playroom, as Granny Tat had called the house's biggest space, lived up to its name, especially on the endless rainy days that interrupted each summer like commas on a page. Dilly remembered pedaling her tricycle down the room's thirty-foot length while wind-whipped sugar maple branches lashed long, rain-spattered windows. She and Sasha still played there, in fact, having pillow-skiing contests—skidding contests, was more like it!—that usually ended either in disaster or gasping hysterics.

Her mom and Libby had probably spent long rainy after-

noons up there too when they were kids, Dilly realized suddenly. So Libby easily might have stashed the dreaded letter
away in the room—for old time's sake. Wide cupboards were
tucked under the steep eaves that sloped over the room's
longest windowless wall, since that space would otherwise
have been wasted; any one of those cupboards would make
an excellent hiding place.

But those hidden shelves were stacked high now with in-
complete jigsaw puzzles, dusty Monopoly sets lacking their
get-out-of-jail-free cards, and long-extinct games that were
missing instruction pamphlets. Could she ever find a simple
envelope there, if that's where Libby had decided to hide it?

Or was the letter down in the pantry, slipped into a child's
raincoat pocket or a cobweb-choked riding boot Libby knew
would remain undisturbed for years on end?

There were so *many* hidden places where her mother's
letter could be!

So it was time to start looking, Dilly told herself.

Chapter Six  **An Elaborate Display of Brittle Brown Leaves**

She spent the rest of the morning in the playroom, methodically searching through its cupboards. As the radio played and a rising sun slowly heated up the pine-paneled room, her strenuous work almost enabled Dilly to forget about the temper tantrum she'd thrown at Libby's house.

Almost.

"How humiliating," Dilly murmured aloud, blushing, as she remembered the morning's scene.

Stacked among the dusty board games she found yellowed lists of dubious words from old Scrabble matches, a few tiny undated and unidentified snapshots of long-dead pets, and—most interesting—an elaborate display of brittle brown leaves pasted onto six pieces of laundry cardboard. Each leaf was identified with both its English and Latin names.

"'Sugar maple: *Acer saccharum*. Black locust: *Robinia pseudoacacia*,'" Dilly said aloud. She stumbled a little over the Latin words.

At the bottom right corner of each piece of cardboard, Dilly's mother had signed her name and written the date in extra-fancy writing: *Elspeth Dillon. July 1973.* Her mom had been—let's see, thirteen years old that summer, Dilly figured, since she was born in 1960.

She'd been almost Dilly's exact same age then.

Well, so what? Some of Dilly's old anger toward her long-absent mother rekindled.

But who knew her mom had been that interested in trees?

Dilly raised her eyes to look out the wide stretch of the room's north-facing windows. A small field—whose modest expanse was interrupted only by the gigantic net-wrapped blueberry bush that fed them each summer—sloped up to meet the forest that continued to rise beyond it. Surrounding the field like a curtain were trees, trees, trees, all green and looking pretty much the same this lush time of year, at least to Dilly. Only the few pale, graceful quaking aspens—called "popples," locally—that shivered at the very front of the other trees stood out in contrast.

So her mother had loved trees. She'd certainly had a lot of leaves to work with.

No, Dilly realized suddenly—this kind of project had Granny Tat written all over it. Granny Tat must have come up with this project to keep her granddaughter busy for a few days. Elspeth Dillon's parents had already been killed in that car accident by then.

"Dilly," Peter Howell shouted from the foot of the stairs. "Lunch in ten minutes."

Dilly returned the leaf display to the top shelf of the last cupboard, closed the door, and got stiffly to her feet. Her hands were filthy. How did everything get so dirty, shut up tight the way it was? "Be right down, Dad," she called out.

She wondered if her mother had ever shown her husband this old project. *"Look what Granny Tat made me do one summer,"* she might have said. Maybe they'd even laughed about it. The leaf project must have meant something, anyway—to someone—or else it wouldn't have been saved.

No, that wasn't necessarily true, Dilly realized. Since her family seemed to have saved everything, maybe the leaf project had meant no more than the old Parcheesi board she'd unearthed an hour earlier.

Someone had squirreled that away, too.

People stashed things away for the strangest reasons— and you never knew who was going to be the next person to look at something you'd saved, Dilly realized suddenly. Standing motionless at the bathroom sink, she let cool water run over her hands as she tried to remember what she'd hidden away in her own room. What would people find if for some terrible reason she never returned to Pasadena?

And what would they *think* about what they'd found?

There was that small plastic bag heavy with sand from La Jolla, the beach resort she'd gone to with her dad on vacation last winter. Dilly must have had the best time in her life then, people would think—when really, she had saved the sand because La Jolla was where she'd been when she started her first period.

And there hadn't been anyone to tell.

What about that collection of Sasha's funniest e-mails? Didn't they prove Sasha Thorne was practically a comedian? Sure, Dilly thought—if you ignored the fact that the other side of Sasha's humor could be dark, dark, dark. She could be moody, too.

Then there were those two notes Jared Herlihy had sent her last year. Dilly must really like him, right? Wrong! Jared made fun of that disabled kid who was being mainstreamed into the other sixth-grade class, so he stood exactly nowhere with Dilly. But the notes were the first ones she'd ever gotten from a boy, so she'd dutifully saved them as part of her history.

Like the Declaration of Independence, only with bad spelling.

And what, Dilly asked herself, about the battered copy of *Pat the Bunny* she'd put away on her top closet shelf, wrapped in one of her mother's old paisley scarves? Pretty tragic, huh? A kid saving a baby book that way, when the mom who used to read it to her was long gone?

Nope, Dilly replied silently, wiping her hands more thoroughly than was necessary.

She just liked *Pat the Bunny*, that was all.

And you couldn't take good enough care of a book you really loved.

❖ ❖ ❖

Dilly's father was in his super-efficient mode at lunch, the way he was at the beginning of each of their summer visits to the farm. "Georgie Thorne did a great job mowing the fields this summer," he said over his shoulder as he cut their tuna sandwiches in half, "but he couldn't get the brush hog close enough to the rocks to get all the saplings. So I'll start in on cutting those down right after lunch. What are you going to do this afternoon?" he asked, wrenching open a jar of sweet pickles. "Want me to run you into town before I get started in the field, so you can go to the library and pick out a few books?"

The library! Libby Thorne's pale, shocked face popped suddenly into Dilly's mind. "Oh, no thanks," Dilly said, pretending to give the matter some thought. "But maybe we can go into Glens Falls tomorrow. They have a much bigger library there, don't forget—that's the one I want to go to. And we can pick up some fruit and stuff at Price Chopper."

Peter Howell took a sip of his iced tea. "Well, okay," he said slowly. "But I want to talk to Libby before too long—invite her over for dinner, maybe. She's done a lot for us, don't forget."

"What—ever," Dilly said coolly, much to her father's surprise.

The upstairs hall was large, as halls go, almost a perfect square, not counting the rectangular area formed by the L of the upstairs banisters. Inside that rectangle sat the big painted chest.

How old was the chest? Dilly didn't know.

What had been its original purpose? Not a clue.

Who had painted it? She didn't know that either, although the chest did not look terribly ancient.

The chest had simply always been there in the hall during Dilly's lifetime—all eight hundred years of it, Dilly thought, smiling a little at the exaggeration.

But why was she grinning? That had been a close call, her dad wanting to take her to the library! She would have to deal with it all—with the quarrel, with Libby—someday, Dilly warned herself.

Not today, though.

Dilly eased back the chest's heavy lid; it seemed to let out a startled squeak of protest. A black chain was supposed to be able to hold the lid open, and Dilly hoped it would work.

A half-dozen mingled smells rose from the opened chest, including the toasty, almost scorched scent of long-ago-ironed linens, musty crocheted blankets, and old French lavender, tucked away between layers of fabric in beribboned sprigs and handkerchief sachets.

No mouse droppings or mildew, though; Marti Oller was too diligent a housekeeper for anything like that, Dilly was relieved to see.

Feeling somewhat like an archaeologist, Dilly lifted out the uppermost layer of neatly folded objects from the chest: embroidered pillow slips and almost-shiny damask tablecloths. Dilly stacked these things carefully at the far end of the hall's blue-painted floor, knowing she'd only have to refold every-thing later or answer to Mrs. Oller if she was sloppy.

The second layer was blankets: three loopy crocheted af-fairs that someone had clearly slaved over; a plaid camp blanket with whip-stitched edges; a couple of scratchy blan-kets with pilled and faded satin bindings; even a child's tat-tered blankie, obviously much-loved, that had been folded into a square.

That was kind of sad, Dilly thought, just as something slid from between the blanket's folds onto the floor.

Dilly almost cried out in triumph. The letter!

But no, what had fallen from the baby blanket was not a let-ter. It was a cardboard box that had once held typing paper. Dilly picked the box up, opened it, and stared for a moment at the topmost piece of paper inside.

"*Dear Libby,*" it began.

Chapter Seven  Dear Libby, Dear Elle

November 28, 1972
Boston

Dear Libby,

Thank you for coming to the funeral. And thanks for not saying anything sad to me afterwards, because I might have actually started crying if you had. Every- one is madly waiting for me to fall apart, but no way is <u>*that*</u> *gonna happen. Not if I can help it, which I can.*

People make me sick, they are such hypocrites. "Poor Hallie. Poor Syb." Well, what did my parents <u>*think*</u> *was gonna happen if they headed south in a straight line down the Taconic Parkway, possibly the world's curviest road? When they'd been* <u>*drinking*</u>*, surprise surprise? Did they think they were magic or something?*

Did they think about <u>*me*</u>*?*

Anyway, Granny Tat is the one who really always took care of me, so nothing much has changed. Except she wants me to go to boarding school in Boston, not Connecticut. Starting next semester, in January.

And here is the best part: She wants you to go with me! Her treat!! She is writing your mom a separate letter, explaining the whole thing.

What about it? It's an all-girls school, but I think it'll be great! We'll have a blast!!

Love,

Little Orphan Elspeth

December 3, 1972

Lake Luzerne

Dear Orphan,

I am just in total shock here. Me, in private school? In Boston? I don't get it. Why can't you just come to the farm during the summer, like before? And we can see each other then!

I mean, I'd like to go to school with you and everything. That would be so rad, and the catalog your grandmother sent looks pretty cool. All those lawns and ivy and stuff. But I wouldn't know how to act around those stuck-up snooty girls, all snobby and everything. I wouldn't even know what to wear. (I know, I know, we would wear uniforms to class! And your grandmother would buy them for us! But what about the rest of the time? Like when it's time to put on our nightgowns? What am I going to wear, my gigantic old T-shirt from Great Escape?)

I don't know, Elle. If anyone in this family should go

*to such a great private school, it's my little brother
Asher. He's the smart one. And I think I would actually
miss his nerdy little self if I had to go away!*

*In other words, I don't want to make you even
more sad or anything, but I'm pretty happy here. I do
miss you, though.*

Love,

Libby

*p.s. My mom absolutely loves the idea of me going
away to school, though. She says it would be the making of me—as if I wasn't already here! What an insult!!*

December 8, 1972

Boston

Dear Libby,

*Hey, are you calling me stuck-up, snobby, and
snooty? Thanks a lot!!! Listen, I visited the school last
week, and it wasn't like that at all. Everybody seemed
pretty nice, even if they did stare at me like I had just
dropped in from the planet Mars.*

*But don't worry, you'll fit in great there. And I have
six Lanz nightgowns, so you won't sprain anyone's eyeballs with that T-shirt of yours. I can lend you a nightgown—or even give one to you. You're welcome!*

This is going to be so cool.

Love,

Elle

p.s. I'm sorry about Asher, but this school is <u>girls</u> <u>only</u>. And anyway, Granny Tat can't send everyone in the whole world to boarding school, can she?

December 11, 1972
Lake Luzerne

Dear Elle,

Listen, I do not <u>want</u> to go to school in Boston. No offense or anything, but I like living at home with my little brother and my mom and dad! I like going to school here in Lake Luzerne! There, I've said it.

And anyway, since your grandmother already lives in Boston, how come she wants you to go to <u>boarding</u> school there? That doesn't make any sense.

I just want things to be the way they were, with you coming here for weekends and the summer, and us being Lake Luzerne friends. Okay??

I know this sounds harsh, but I would feel like your pet or something if your grandmother paid for me to go to school with you in Boston. So let's stop talking about it. But I will send you my famous cookies when you're there, so you will make other friends <u>for</u> <u>sure</u>!!

Love,
Libby

December 13, 1972
Boston

Libby—

   First of all, Granny Tat wants me nearer than Con-
necticut but not actually in her house. She's worried
that I won't "thrive," as she puts it (like I was one of her
prize-winning African violets) if I'm not around other
girls. And she wanted to make sure I had at least one
friend there, which is where you were supposed to
come in. Ha ha.

   Second, things just aren't the way they were. For
me, especially. I didn't think I'd have to explain that.
Thanks for reminding me, though.

   Third, if I was gonna get a pet, I'd get one who was
a lot more loyal to me than you are being right now!!

   This whole thing was not my idea, don't forget.
And it's not exactly like I was asking you to go to jail
with me, or something. This is a very nice school we're
talking about.

   Look—just forget the whole thing, okay? I'm sorry
I ever mentioned it. See you around.

Elle

p.s. And don't bother sending any cookies, thanks. I'm
sure we'll have plenty of fancier stuff to eat.

December 16, 1972
Lake Luzerne

Dear Mrs. Dillon,

   Thank you so much for your generous offer to send Elizabeth (Libby) off to school with Elspeth next month! We have given the matter a great deal of thought, and after visiting the school, and meeting with its very impressive headmistress, we have decided to accept your offer on Libby's behalf.

   This will mean so much to Libby in her future life! I know she'll make us proud.

   She joins us in sending her thanks, of course.

   Love to Elspeth.

                    Sincerely,
                    Mr. and Mrs. A. Durand Thorne

Chapter Eight  What's Going On?

Wow, Dilly thought—her mom had been a selfish kid! A spoiled brat, too, if a person could be spoiled when her parents were dead. But Elspeth Dillon had definitely gotten her own way when she wanted something—such as having Libby attend boarding school with her.

Kind of like a tame friend. Or a pet, as Libby had put it.

Because even if it had been Granny Tat's idea to start with, Elle had jumped right in, saying *"It'll be great!"* as if the whole thing were already settled, regardless of what Libby wanted.

Poor Libby.

Draping the paisley scarf miniskirt-like across her lap, Dilly leaned against the wall and reviewed the few things she knew about Libby Thorne's life—after the boarding school thing. College somewhere in New York, then a quick marriage. Unhappy, according to Sasha. No kids. She had taken back her maiden name, Sasha said.

Libby was a librarian, so she must have trained to do that after college, in other words after she was married. But then what had happened? Why had she gotten a divorce? Had her husband had an affair with another woman? Or maybe he just hadn't liked living with a librarian. Had Libby fined her husband a nickel a day for not putting his dirty dishes in the sink, for instance, or *shhhh*'d him once too often for making noise in the morning?

Who knew? Not Sasha, for once.

And who knew how Libby's life would have differed if she hadn't been marched off to boarding school in Boston? Perhaps she would have met the love of her life during her senior year of regular high school—in Lake Luzerne. She might not have gone to college and become a librarian, true, but maybe she would have.

Libby would have had three or four kids by now, though— all girls, Dilly imagined, and looking like white-blond dandelion puffs as they romped near the river in their clean little frocks.

Girls often wore frocks in storybooks, and Libby's would have been the perfect storybook family; Dilly was sure of it.

So basically, Dilly thought, her mom had ruined Libby's life as well as hers, Dilly's, and maybe even deprived Libby of a family—without even giving the matter a second thought. Dilly's old, carefully nourished resentment flared, as if someone had just tossed a new log onto an invisible fire.

Really, she reassured herself, what she had *said* to Libby that morning was nothing—nothing!—compared to what her mom had *done* to Libby. Doing was always worse than saying, wasn't it?

Again, poor Libby. Had she returned to Lake Luzerne right

after her divorce, or did she plod through a few miserable years in the city, alone? Years when Elle had pranced off to live her own life—in California, with handsome Peter Howell?

"I'm done with you. You're on your own, now," Dilly imagined her mother telling a newly single Libby Thorne over the phone.

Sasha. *She's* the one who should hear this story, Dilly told herself.

"Hey, Sasha," she said a couple of minutes later. She scrunched the telephone receiver between her ear and shoulder as she tried to make her bed—while she was still sitting on it. It didn't work.

"Dilly," Sasha Thorne said, not sounding one bit surprised to be hearing from her friend, although they rarely phoned each other. "What's the matter? What's going on? I was just about to call you."

"You were?" Dilly asked, pleased.

"What's *happening*? Are you okay?"

I'm fine," Dilly said. But she was thinking, *Uh-oh.*

Because for a moment, she had completely forgotten about her fight with Libby! That fight was a fact, though, a done deal, Dilly scolded herself, her mind racing. And there was no escaping it—or its consequences. But if her fight with Libby slopped over onto her friendship with Sasha, Libby's niece? Then where would she be? Friendless in the Adirondacks, that's where.

And if the fight spread, Dilly thought, her mind racing, perhaps Libby's uncle would decide to stop mowing the fields, and what was left of the farm would quickly be overgrown. There would be this huge storm, and gnarly old trees would crash to the ground.

Then the Thorne who was a plumber wouldn't drain the pipes correctly for the winter, out of spite, and they would burst with the thaw, and the ceilings—and perhaps the entire house!—would cave in and be ruined forever.

All thanks to her, Dilly.

"Aunt Libby called," Sasha said, confirming Dilly's worst fears. "She said you could use a friend right about now. What's that supposed to mean? *Are you all right?*"

Sasha was a secret worrier, Dilly knew from several years' e-mail correspondence. She worried like crazy whenever her parents had a fight, for instance, even though they didn't have a *clue*. "I told you, Sash, I'm fine. And I never meant for Libby to—"

"But then why does she want me to come up there?" Sasha asked, plowing right through Dilly's hesitant attempt at apology.

"You're coming up? That's great, Sasha. When are you getting here?"

"Late Friday afternoon," Sasha said, clearly annoyed about something. "Aunt Libby's going to pick me up at the Amtrak station in Saratoga Springs. But that's not the point. The point is, you know I'll always be there for you, if you need me. But you *don't*. So why does my aunt want me up there *now*, if you're really okay?"

"Don't you want to come?" Dilly asked, puzzled—and a little hurt.

Because if Sasha didn't want to see her, then she didn't want to see Sasha!

"Well yeah, I want to come—eventually. I want to see you this summer, of course," Sasha told her, impatient. "Only there's a lot of stuff going on here right now. I had *plans*, Dilly. And anyway, I was going to come up to Lake Luzerne closer to your birthday, for a *whole week*. We would have had a great time. But now I'm supposed to drop everything and ditch my friends and haul myself onto a slow train heading north? How come? Is my *aunt* okay?"

"She's fine. Everything's perfectly fine," Dilly reassured Sasha, her heart thudding as she told the lie. "Look, I'm sorry Libby's dragging you up here, but it's not because of me. You don't think I asked her to make you come, do you?" she asked.

And she thought suddenly of Granny Tat and Elspeth Dillon and Boston, in 1972.

"I guess you didn't," Sasha admitted.

"It's not like I need somebody up here to entertain me," Dilly continued, her voice stiff. "Maybe your aunt just misses you, Sasha."

"Maybe. So what's up?"

"Huh?"

"How come you called?" Sasha asked, enunciating each word in an infuriating way. "Did you want me to check your e-mail for you?"

"Maybe later," Dilly said, quickly going over what she'd planned on telling Sasha—and throwing out most of it.

Because perhaps now wasn't the best time to talk about how Libby had had to change her life and go away to school in Boston just because Granny Tat was worried about Elspeth being lonely. Wasn't there kind of a similarity with this situation, although it happened so long ago? Sasha was being summoned to Lake Luzerne because Libby was worried about her, Dilly. Was history repeating itself today, the way people said it did?

She hadn't meant for anything like this to happen!

"So why did you call?" Sasha asked again.

"I just wanted to say hi," Dilly said, realizing how lame that sounded.

There was a brief impatient silence, during which Dilly could almost see her friend peel a glittering slice of polish from her nail and flick it across the room. "Well, hi and bye. I gotta go," Sasha said at last. "You can say hi to me again on Friday, okay? A million times, if you want to. I'll probably be up there long enough."

"Lucky me," Dilly said, trying to sound cool.

Hey, she thought—if Sasha could be that way, so could she!

Chapter Nine  Saratoga Springs

Dilly's father insisted that they take the next day off and drive down to Saratoga Springs for a treat. They would browse through the shops, he said, have lunch at some snazzy place, and maybe pick up a ballet schedule. The New York City Ballet performed there in an outdoors amphitheater for several weeks each summer, and Dilly and her dad always tried to go at least once.

Because Mummie had loved the ballet.

Dilly was almost positive that Libby hadn't called her dad yet to tell him about the letter from her mom—if she ever *was* going to call. Not wanting to think about this, Dilly settled back into what was left of their forty-minute ride and watched the trees, fields, and white clapboard houses zip by.

It was good to get out of Lake Luzerne, Dilly told herself. It was almost as though she could leave her worries behind— worries about Sasha, mostly.

Now, everything else seemed less important than the mysterious quarrel they'd had. Even the thought of that dreaded letter from her mom had become like the spooky mists that rose from the Hudson and faded into the air each morning, while the fight she'd had with Sasha seemed to hang in that very air. And the bad feelings weren't going anywhere.

Why, Dilly asked herself, did Sasha's friendship mean so much to her? Was it because Sasha was the only kid she knew in Lake Luzerne? That was partly it, Dilly admitted. But it was also because Sasha—her sour pickle of a friend!—was special.

She was honest and loyal, for instance. What about that time a few years back when Dilly had almost buried herself alive, thanks to a digging miscalculation? Lost that summer in a *Wind in the Willows* imaginary world she'd allowed only Sasha—Mr. Toad, to Dilly's Ratty—to share, Dilly hollowed out a burrow from a crumbling dirt bank alongside an unusually low Hudson River.

She'd dug too deep into the bank, however, and it partially collapsed on top of her. Sasha grabbed an arm and hauled her out of the frightening muck before Dilly even knew what had happened.

And Sasha never blabbed, even though she'd been a hero. "You'd be grounded for the rest of your life if your dad ever found out," she'd said, shaking her head.

And another thing: Sasha was absolutely unshockable. After all, Dilly reminded herself, couldn't she say things to Sasha she could never say to Becka or Fran?

Or to *anyone*?

Becka and Fran were almost paralyzed by the thought that Dilly didn't have a mother, for instance, while Sasha didn't seem to care. She didn't think Dilly was weird at all. She had even said that Dilly was lucky *not* to have a mom, once or twice.

Dilly was able to be honest with Sasha, until yesterday's phone call, anyway. She could tell Sasha that it honestly didn't matter all that much about her mom being dead, because she couldn't really remember her.

But she could also tell Sasha the things about not having a mom that made her angry. Dilly could say how she knew it was a little crazy being mad at her mom for dying, but that that had been her first reaction as a six-year-old to the terrible news, and she was kind of stuck with it. Sasha didn't mind—or try to make things all better.

Becka would probably think she *was* crazy if she, Dilly, said she was mad at her mother sometimes, and Fran would try to reassure Dilly, telling her that she didn't really feel that way at all.

But Sasha didn't argue, and Sasha didn't care how mad Dilly got at her mom. Sasha had always gotten angry right along with Dilly!

So how could she, Dilly, not be worried, now that Sasha seemed to be so angry?

Because where did that leave her?

❖   ❖   ❖

Saratoga Springs was an old-fashioned New York town that was not typical of other towns its size, at least in the summer. It had been a spa town—because of the famous health-enhancing springs—for over a hundred and fifty years. Huge hotels had once catered to crowds of health seekers, many of whom returned each year. Some of these old hotels were still standing.

Instead of the usual handful of mansions belonging to rich merchants that might be found tucked away on one or two shady side streets in a similar town, Saratoga Springs boasted many such nineteenth-century dwellings. By now, some of them had been reconfigured inside to create space for more than one family, and many of the town's bigger houses rented rooms by the week each August, at the peak of the summer season. The Saratoga horse racing track operated for the entire month, then, and the town's streets were almost overwhelmed by traffic and excitement.

"It looks just the same as always," Dilly observed as they drove down Broadway.

"Crowded, for a Tuesday—even in July. And hot," her dad chimed in as usual.

It was true; Saratoga Springs was usually a good ten degrees warmer than the village of Lake Luzerne, which was surrounded by trees and at a slightly higher elevation. The Howells usually returned home headachy and exhausted.

And that was just silly, Dilly thought, because Pasadena

was at least five times bigger than Saratoga Springs. She never got tired in Pasadena.

"Where do you want to have lunch, Dilly?" her father asked. She always got to select the place.

Dilly peered up at the Fourth-of-July bunting that still decorated many storefronts and listened to her stomach growl. Choosing the restaurant was a big decision to make during these summer visits, because she and her dad might not dine out again for a week or more.

In Pasadena, they often went out to eat; there were dozens upon dozens of places to choose from. Dilly liked that.

"How about the Adelphi?" Dilly's father suggested, naming one of the few remaining old hotels. "Their little garden restaurant out back was one of Mummie's favorite places."

Scratch the Adelphi, Dilly thought mulishly, although she too loved going there—when she was wearing a dress, anyway. She liked to arrange her skirt "just so" on the wrought iron chair and pretend that she was a girl living back in the olden days. An heiress, maybe—but the *fun* kind, not the type of heiress who was stuck with an old house in the middle of nowhere, who had a neighbor who was mad at her and one friend who didn't even want to talk to her, and who was surrounded by a million trees that never stopped growing, shedding their leaves, and crashing to the ground during winter storms.

"Let's go someplace completely different," Dilly said, and

so they parked the car and made their way down the sidewalk past window-shoppers and the stony-faced groups of older teens who clustered on steps and in doorways like small flocks of ill-tempered crows. "Here," Dilly said suddenly, and she and her dad veered into one of the several new restaurants that had appeared on Broadway since the previous summer.

Their sandwiches were slow in coming. Around them, women chattered animatedly in groups of two, three, or four, maneuvering forkfuls of chicken salad or glistening berry tart toward their mouths, which never seemed to stop moving. Her dad was just about the sole man in the restaurant, Dilly observed, and they were the only ones not talking. "So, how did Mummie and Granny Tat get to be so bossy?" she heard herself ask her father.

Startled at the sound of her own voice, and horrified at the question she'd just asked, Dilly busied herself trying to take a sip of her iced tea. The glass bristled with a mint sprig, lemon wedge, straw, and a tall spoon she'd forgotten to remove, though, and she poked herself in the nose.

Dilly's father frowned. "Wow, Dilly-dill," he said quietly. "Where did *that* come from?"

Dilly managed a tiny shrug. "It's just a question," she mumbled. "You don't have to answer it."

"Oh, honey—of course I'll answer it," her dad said. "You

have every right to ask me questions about your mother. In fact, I want you to," he added, too obviously trying to paste an encouraging look upon his suddenly gloomy face.

"I only wondered," Dilly said, trying to look bored. "It just seems like each of them got her way most of the time."

At the next table, a woman fished something out of a glossy pink shopping bag and then held an intricately smocked baby dress tenderly to her chest. The other women at the table leaned forward, enraptured.

Peter Howell looked thoughtful. "Well, Granny Tat usually got her way," he conceded. "She came from an extremely privileged background, don't forget, and she had a forceful personality, so she was used to people falling in line with whatever she wanted. It just sort of seemed like the natural thing to do. Your mother always tried to avoid going head-to-head with her, that's for sure."

"They were all snobs," Dilly said, her heart pounding as she uttered the words. "Everyone in Lake Luzerne says so."

"They do?" Dilly's dad said, not looking especially disturbed. "Well, Granny Tat was definitely a snob. And I suppose if I were being perfectly honest, I'd have to say that Elspeth was maybe a *bit* of a snob too," he admitted. "But only in a way. How could she not be one, having being raised as she was? By the time I met Elle, though, she had been on her own for a while—working in Boston, but meeting people whose families her grandmother had never heard of. And Elle loved every minute of her new life."

"She was still snobbish, though."

"Not about money," her father said, trying to sort out his thoughts. "Mummie was miles away from Granny Tat on that subject, although Granny Tat herself used to laugh out loud at the current notion that it's how much money a person earns that determines his or her so-called class. Not that I ever heard her use such an expression. But Granny Tat would have been much more curious about a person's family background, or—sorry to say it—their trust fund, than your mother ever was. *'It's not merely a matter of what you have, it's what you're able to keep down through the generations that really counts,'* Granny Tat used to say. *'Any yahoo can make money.' "*

Dilly stirred her iced tea. "Well, what about Mummie?" she asked. "What was she curious about when she met a person?"

"Oh, how creative they were, maybe. Or their manners. You know, how kind they were to other people. And a sense of humor mattered a lot to Elle. Of course, that usually goes along with intelligence."

Dilly frowned. "I like funny people, too. But how is that being a snob?"

"I'm not putting this right," Dilly's father said, frustrated. "I guess I should have said she was a kind of *reverse* snob, maybe."

"What do you mean?"

Peter Howell thought a moment. "Well, for instance, Elle was huge, just huge, on maintenance," he said. "She always giggled at all the so-called yuppies we knew who bought brand-new everything, but then didn't know enough to take care of their possessions. She herself didn't mind it a bit when things got a little run-down—especially at the farm. In fact, she would much rather spend two thousand dollars patching up the living room walls there and keeping the old wallpaper that had been up for the last fifty years than spend one thousand dollars to get the whole thing completely done over."

"Huh," Dilly said. She had often wondered about that funky blue wallpaper. She kind of liked it, though.

"And when the old yellow station wagon we had up here finally gave out," her father continued, "Elle wouldn't hear of us buying a new car. Not a chance, she said. She insisted that Mr. Pickens would find us a perfectly good used one at auction. *'Perfectly good.'* That was pure Dillon, and pure Elle. She was a 'perfectly good' snob, you could say."

The table was quiet for a few seconds as Peter Howell took a big bite of his sandwich. Dilly had been hungry when they'd walked into the restaurant, but now she felt a little queasy. "But Daddy," she finally burst out. "You *love* having a really nice car at home. So isn't it kind of fakey not to get one here, if you can afford it?"

Peter Howell threw back his head and laughed, and the women sitting nearest them gave him some admiring glances. "You are definitely your mother's daughter, Dilly," he said. "She always loved a good argument, too. I guess you're a reverse-reverse snob."

❖ ❖ ❖

"You are definitely your mother's daughter."

The words seemed to echo in Dilly's ears. She wanted more than anything to argue with her father, but she couldn't imagine where to begin.

She might say, *"I'm not like her at all. She was a snob, and I'm not. Not even a reverse-reverse one."*

Or, *"I'm not like her at all. She belonged up here, and I don't."*

Or, *"I'm not like her at all. If I died, I would never come back from the grave and try to keep bossing everyone around!"*

Or, *"I'm not like my mother at all. She's dead, and I'm alive."*

Instead, however, Dilly picked up her sandwich and prepared to take her first bite.

After all, this was supposed to be a treat, wasn't it?

Chapter Ten  **Sorting Through Your Dead Mother's Clothes**

"I was thinking I would go through some of the junk around here this summer," Dilly said at breakfast the next morning. "It's been piling up for years."

The stricken look that flitted across her father's face made Dilly feel as though her heart were shrinking a little, but her dad composed himself a split second later. "Good idea," he said.

"I would never throw out anything of Mummie's," Dilly tried to reassure him.

Her father sighed. "Maybe it's time. Maybe we *should* toss out a few things while we're here, or give them away. It's a shame to have things go to waste if somebody can use them. The historical society is always holding some tag sale or other. So is the library, for that matter." He brightened a little, having mentioned the library.

The blasted library again. *Libby*. Dilly frowned.

She and her dad were silent for a minute or two, while Dilly tried desperately not to think about Libby. Instead, she tried to picture just what Lake Luzerne possessions of her mother's might be given away. What about the clothes that still hung neatly spaced in her bedroom closet and lay folded in her bureau drawers? The square, airy room had once been Great aunt LillyDill's bedroom; the old rose-patterned paper, faded, puckered, and curling in places, gave the space a distinctly feminine air, though Elspeth and Peter had shared it for nine summers.

That room was like a shrine, now, and used only when the house was full of guests. Peter Howell had moved his things into the farm's smallest bedroom the summer following his wife's death. Although it was a white, uncurtained, spartan space with no closet, he said it suited him just fine.

Could Dilly give away the yellowing paperbacks—mostly mysteries—that her mother had enjoyed when she was a teenager, or the magazines she'd been reading that last summer spent here? Her father might miss those books and magazines less than the clothes.

How about throwing away the leaf project?

No, Dilly thought—she could never do that. *She* liked the leaf project, now.

It was difficult discarding anything at the farm, she realized. Objects seemed to take on personalities of their own—perhaps over the winter—as the years passed: stacks of old *House and Garden* magazines formed families; cooking implements gathered in little communities.

Mrs. Oller straightened and dusted it all without comment.

"Could *you* give away Mummie's clothes for me, Dilly?" Peter Howell asked softly, staring at his folded hands. "I could ask Marti to take care of it, if you'd rather. Or Libby." He looked a little more cheerful again.

"No. I'll do it," Dilly said hastily. "If you're sure."

Her father nodded. "I'm sure," he said.

Sorting through your dead mother's clothes had to be the worst way in the world to start the day, Dilly thought at ten o'clock. But it was raining outside, and her dad was working in his garage workshop; he wouldn't come bursting into the room on some pretext and get all sad and everything.

Dilly knew that she could get out of performing this sorry task without too much trouble, but Mrs. Oller wasn't coming for another few days, and Dilly was afraid that her father— having finally decided he was ready for this momentous thing to happen—would not want to wait that long for the grim chore to be done.

It had been just the opposite at home, taking Peter Howell only a month to empty his wife's closet after her death. Dilly still remembered the shock she'd felt, returning home from a sad weekend trip with her dad to Laguna Beach, to find— when sneaking into her mother's closet for a furtive nestle among familiar garments—that everything was gone.

Her father had asked Elle's friends to come in while they were gone to take all her clothes away.

Dilly definitely did not want her father asking Libby Thorne to carry out the task here at the farm. That would get them talking, and then she, Dilly, would be really and truly busted—because her father would find out how rude she'd been to Libby.

And the one thing her dad would not tolerate was bad manners.

But she was pretty safe, Dilly told herself. Libby was busy at the library, and her dad was kept occupied doing chores and keeping her, Dilly, entertained. She had everything under control.

The muffled sound of rain seemed to surround Dilly in the dim light of her mother's room; it was like being inside a cocoon. The room was stuffy, though. Dilly wrestled open the window a bit, let in some damp, leaf-scented air, and took a deep breath.

Green, Dilly thought: You could almost see the color as moist air floated in past the limp, dispirited-looking dotted Swiss curtains framing her mother's window.

There had been no closet in the room at all when the farmhouse had been built. Clothes were stored in chests at first, Dilly supposed, or hung in armoires, or kept folded in bureau drawers. A small closet had been added to one corner of the bedroom around the time of Granny Tat's wedding to Blainey Dillon, however. That had been in 1928, Dilly remembered having heard.

In fact, the back of the closet was still covered by the

room's original wallpaper, still surprisingly bright. Dilly tried to imagine all the clothes that had brushed against that paper: fringed roaring-twenties dresses; droopy Depression-era clothes from the thirties; patriotic wartime outfits from the forties; poodle skirts from the fifties.

Emptying her mother's clothes from that tiny closet was easy. Dilly simply opened the closet door, shut her eyes, and gathered all the garments together in one quick movement. Sun dresses, brightly patterned summer skirts, dressy pants, and shirts still in their clear dry cleaning bags were unceremoniously crushed together, after having enjoyed six years' undisturbed repose.

Some of this stuff was still okay looking, and it might even fit *her* by now, Dilly realized as she clasped the clothes in her arms. But no way would she wear any of it; that would be just too weird.

And anyway, her poor dad would probably faint if she were to come prancing down the stairs in one of her mother's old outfits. Or he might have a heart attack, and then where would she be? She couldn't bear even to think about that.

With some effort, Dilly manhandled the hangers off the sagging rod, then she staggered over to the bed and let her mom's clothes flop onto the white chenille spread. She quickly folded the pile of clothing—still on hangers—into untidy thirds, then jammed everything into one of the big cardboard boxes she'd brought upstairs with a few empty plastic grocery bags just after breakfast.

"There. That's done," Dilly told herself encouragingly, and she nudged the heavy box toward the door with the side of one leg. "Now for the bureau."

This was turning out to be easier than she'd thought.

Dilly's parents had somehow managed to share the room's one chest of drawers during their marriage, but her mother's clothes seemed to have rearranged themselves into every available space when Peter Howell moved his things out of the room six years earlier. Dilly paused, though, as she was about to open the narrow top drawer.

The lingerie drawer.

Hold it—she shouldn't start there, Dilly told herself. Underwear was just too personal. No kid should have to handle her mother's bras and underpants!

Tears of self-pity filled her green eyes in an instant, and Dilly blinked them angrily away. She decided to start in on the bottom drawer instead.

Dilly realized that she could simply close her eyes again and scoop everything out of each of the bureau's four drawers, but suddenly, this no longer seemed to be the right approach to take. Perhaps the fragrance that Dilly smelled as soon as she opened the bottom drawer was what made her hesitate. The slightly spicy blend of carnations, rosemary, and lavender caused Dilly to sink back on her heels. Her mother had shunned perfume, Dilly knew from family lore, so this fragrance must be coming from the sweaters themselves: the scratchy, sherbet-colored Shetlands, the slippery ivory cashmere with the pearl buttons, the heathery twin-sets, the bulky white cable-knit fisherman's sweater her mother had bought on a trip to Ireland. Or perhaps sachets tucked into the sweaters' woolen folds were the source of that memory-jogging smell.

Dilly reached out and touched the sweater on top of the nearest pile. Its surface felt a little stiff, as if the unimaginably cold days and nights of six long winters in an unheated house had had some lingering effect.

She was afraid to risk unfolding the sweaters. Would they fall apart in her arms? Might squirming larvae drop into her lap or hundreds of moths come flapping out and fly right into her face? The thought was terrifying.

"Good-bye, sweaters," Dilly said abruptly, and she gingerly lifted each of the three stacks out of the bottom drawer and placed it in another cardboard box.

The next drawer—folded Levis, khakis, and shorts—was easier to cope with, for some reason, as was the shirt drawer above it. Dilly's mother had organized that drawer so her snug black and white T-shirts were to the left, brightly colored T-shirts and polo shirts were in the middle, and slouchy turtlenecks were to the right. "You're outta here," Dilly whispered to the shirts, filling the cardboard box almost to the top.

She stood up and stretched, listening to the rain patter down on the roof. Outside, the leaves of a big sugar maple thrashed intermittently, as if the tree were irritably straightening its stiff taffeta skirts.

❖   ❖   ❖

There were three kinds of memories that you could have about a dead person, Dilly thought, staring out at the leaves. First, there were the things others told you that you must surely remember, but you absolutely didn't. These were un-memories, in Dilly's opinion.

"Do you recall how Mummie used to let you brush her hair?"

Nope.

"Don't you remember how Elspeth used to sing to you, Dilly?"

Uh-uh.

"You remember that time you and Mummie got all dressed up, don't you, and she took you to that tea room where people could try on old-fashioned hats? She said you looked so adorable that she just about couldn't stand it!"

Sorry. Not ringing any bells.

Next, there were the things that you didn't remember at all, except through photographs. These eventually became what Dilly thought of as bossy memories. The pictures served as evidence that you had indeed been there, so you *had to* remember.

Exhibit One: Here is Mrs. Peter Howell leaving the hospital on August twenty-first, tired but radiant, cradling her new-born infant, Miss Dillon Halliburton Howell. We've set a record, folks: the longest name for the smallest baby!

Exhibit Two: Here is Mummie wearing a paper hat and carrying a chocolate cake at Dilly's fourth birthday party.

Slender and summer-tanned, Elspeth Howell looks as though she is about fifteen years old, tops, roughly half her actual age. She appears to be singing "Happy Birthday."

She looks very happy.

Dilly is barefoot in this photograph, and that's a funny story: It seems that she was always eager to learn to tie her own shoes, and Mummie told her not to worry, she'd be able to do it when she was four. And so Dilly awoke before dawn the morning of her fourth birthday, ran into her closet, put on a pair of shoes, and—nothing! She still couldn't tie them.

Little Dilly refused to wear shoes for three whole days.

Exhibit Three: This is a picture of Dilly and Mummie curled up on the sofa, watching a video. Mummie is wearing a scarf around her head that makes her look like a fortune-teller, and Dilly has tried to tie a little gingham scarf around her head, too, to copy Mummie. Dilly must be about five years old in this picture. She is watching the TV screen, and Mummie is watching Dilly.

Years later, Dilly remembered every inch of every photograph she and her mother were in together, though not the events pictured in those photographs. This secretly made her wonder if she were the same person that she had been then.

Would Mummie even recognize her now?

The final kind of memories you could have about a dead person, Dilly thought, were what you truly—and privately—remembered. But these could be such odd things! It was almost as though a video camera had clicked on and off at random moments during your life with whoever it was you were trying to remember, and blam, *those* were the things you were stuck with. Not that they necessarily meant anything.

"Trot-trot to Boston, trot-trot to Lynn." Dilly could see the curve of her mother's pretty smile as she recited the old rhyme.

"Always sco-o-o-o-t your chair back under the table before you leave the dining room, Dilly-dilly. That's the ticket!" Dilly remembered a coaxing tilt to her mother's head, and the wing of dark hair that swung over her shoulder.

"I despise one-ply toilet paper. I will not have it in my house." Wow, what was up with that?

"Never interrupt Mummie when she's using the telephone, Dilly." This had been spoken *by* her mother, Dilly recalled, which was confusing—as if sometimes Mummie could be two people at the same time.

Dilly also remembered her mother's bedroom door slamming shut back in California one terrible afternoon, and she could still hear the gulping sobs that came from behind that closed door. The wind was blowing outside, which was also scary, and an integral part of the memory, and eucalyptus nuts rattled against the windows like bony fingers knocking, knocking to get in.

Dilly remembered crouching in the hall, chewing at her fist while she waited for her father to come home. Every detail of that hallway was still clear to her: the chipped baseboard paint where the vacuum cleaner banged against the wall; the intricate geometric pattern of the narrow Persian carpet; the blank recessed panels of her mother's heavy bedroom door.

Dilly had always wanted to draw pictures in those inviting empty spaces.

"That was then, this is now," Dilly told herself sternly, turning back to her mother's bureau.

Only one more drawer to go.

"Okay. This is *totally* no big deal," Dilly reassured herself, and she tried to open the top bureau drawer as though her mother were still alive and had asked Dilly to fetch something for her. A slip, maybe.

Panties were on the left, bras on the right, and her mother's slips and scarves were stacked in a neat silken square in the middle of the drawer.

Dilly held her breath for a moment as she stared at Elspeth Dillon's most intimate clothing. Her mother had loved to splurge on pretty underwear, too, Dilly realized—just the way *she* did! And that was so completely unexpected. Surely the proper Miss Elspeth Dillon had grown up wearing white cotton panties and ribby white undershirts.

Here, though, was a glimpse of the real Elle: bikini-cut panties in shell pink, coffee, and black; matching lace-edged bras trimmed with the tiniest satin ribbons imaginable.

A shiver went down Dilly's back. "Mummie," she said aloud.

Suddenly, Dilly realized that she didn't want to give away her mother's underwear to strangers. She grabbed a couple of plastic grocery bags and began to empty the lingerie drawer into them. She would double-bag the underwear so that her dad would never be able to guess what was inside, Dilly told herself, and then she'd simply throw the bags away.

Out with the garbage. Piece of cake.

The panties went into the first bag, and the bras went into the second. Dilly knotted each bag firmly at the top and then tossed it in the direction of the bedroom door.

That left only the slips and scarves to dispose of, and Dilly decided to tuck those into the second cardboard box. Then she'd be done.

Some papers fluttered out from between two of the scarves, drifting to the floor like autumn leaves.

Dilly was surprised her heart kept on beating.

Chapter Eleven  Add Sugar Gradually

Dilly picked up the two pieces of paper—a yellow-edged sheet that had been ripped from a spiral binder and a single page that had been torn from a kitchen pad—and went over to her mother's bed. She settled onto the bumpy white bedspread, tugged her mom's pillows into a nice soft wedge behind her back, and scanned the pages, searching in vain for a "Dear Dilly."

LIBBY'S COOKIES FOR KIDS WHO JUST CAN'T DECIDE

> 1 stick butter, softened
>
> 3 Tablespoons peanut butter (smooth or crunchy)
>
> $1/2$ cup granulated sugar
>
> $1/3$ cup brown sugar (packed; light or dark)
>
> 1 egg
>
> $1/2$ teaspoon vanilla
>
> 1 cup flour
>
> $1/2$ teaspoon baking soda
>
> 1 six-ounce package chocolate chips
>
> $1/2$ cup oats

$^1\!/_2$ cup dry-roasted peanuts (split them if you want,
  but don't bother to chop)

Directions:

Cream butter and peanut butter. Add sugar gradually and beat until fluffy. Add egg and vanilla.

Mix together flour and baking soda. Add to butter
mixture and stir a few times with a spoon.

Add oats and stir a few more times. Add chocolate
chips and stir some more. Add peanuts and finish stir-
ring.

Drop from teaspoon two inches apart on greased
cookie sheet. Bake at 350° for 12–15 minutes.

Hmm. That must be the recipe for those "famous" cookies
Libby had talked about in her letter—the ones she'd tried to
bribe her friend Elle with, Dilly thought, peering curiously at
the kitten-decorated page torn from the memo pad. The writing was her mom's, though; Dilly recognized it now.

Chocolate chips, oatmeal, peanut butter *and* dry-roasted,
salty peanuts.

Obviously, her mother had wanted to save the recipe.
Maybe she didn't want to forget her fight with Libby, for some
reason. Or else she just really, really liked these cookies.

Dilly's stomach gurgled a little, and she wondered what
they tasted like. Kind of peculiar, she suspected. Had Libby
been the kind of kid who wanted to act different just to stand
out? She didn't seem like that—now, anyway.

Dilly reached next for the sheet of notebook paper.

WHAT MY FUTURE HUSBAND WILL BE LIKE!

by Elspeth Dillon
July 1973
Written in Lake Luzerne, on yet another rainy day

First of all, I won't get married unless I fall in love. Second of all, I won't fall in love until I'm good and ready to. (Unless it's love at first sight, and then I will be SWEPT AWAY. Which I kind of do want to happen, but I kind of don't.)

So, here goes!

Number One: He must be handsome. He has to be taller than I am, and have sexy eyes, and long hair. (I'm not just being selfish here, but if he looks good, our kids will look good, too. Assuming we have any, which is a whole other question.)

Number Two: He must be smart. Partly so we will have smart kids, but also so that he won't be boring. Oh, and he should be funny, too. Because when you get married, it's for a long, long time. You might as well have some laughs!

Number Three: He must be cool. We definitely have to like the same music, and I have to like the way he dresses or it will drive me absolutely nuts.

Number Four: He must have nice manners—or it will

*drive Granny Tat nuts. Well, me too, to tell the truth. (I
mean, if he hunches over his food or chews with his
mouth open, who wants to eat?)*

*<u>Number Five</u>: He must not try to boss me around. He'd
better not even try!!! Because I hate bossy people.*

*<u>Number Six</u>: He must be healthy. I don't want to have
to take care of someone who has the sniffles all of the
time.*

*<u>Number Seven</u>: He must be a person who likes to give
presents. (To me!!!)*

*<u>Number Eight</u>: He must like my friends. Especially
Libby Thorne, even though she is trying to peek over
my shoulder right now.*

<u>Number Nine</u>: He must be a good kisser.

Written at the bottom of this list, in handwriting that Dilly now
recognized as Libby's, was the following:

WHAT <u>MY</u> FUTURE HUSBAND WILL BE LIKE!!

by Libby Thorne
July 1973
Also written in Lake Luzerne

   *MY husband will be exactly the same! Only hand-
somer, smarter, cooler, sexier, and the best kisser in
the whole wide world. A better kisser than Elle's hus-*

band, anyway, and I know that for a fact. But don't ask
me how!!!

Dilly found that she was smiling. Although written thirty years ago, this was just the sort of crazy, teasing thing she and Sasha might come up with to make an endless rainy afternoon pass quicker.

Her mom sounded like—like such a *kid*.

And how weird, her mom saying that she hated bossy people—when she, Elspeth, was already that way, at age . . . thirteen, Dilly guessed, figuring quickly. Also, that whole part about how her husband had to be so healthy and everything was kind of creepy. After all, Peter Howell—*short-haired* Peter Howell—was the one who'd ended up taking care of Elle until she died.

Elle.

Elspeth.

Elspeth Halliburton Dillon.

Elspeth Halliburton Dillon Howell.

Elspeth Halliburton Dillon Howell (deceased).

No matter what you called her, she was in Dilly's thoughts for long moments each day, and Dilly resented it. Why did her mother still matter so much, Dilly asked herself, when she'd been dead for six years?

But it was as though there were a mom-shaped hole in her heart, she confessed to herself now.

Dilly shut her eyes and began her own list, a list of reasons why she was so mad at her mother—although really, she couldn't even remember what she looked like, not without peeking at a photograph first.

One: She was mean to Libby.

Well, that wasn't really very fair, Dilly admitted silently. The whole thing about going to boarding school in Boston had just kind of happened, courtesy of the grown-ups involved, and she had only now learned about it. So why put it on the list?

Also, hadn't she, Dilly, been just as mean to Libby? Or even meaner?

Dilly hastily went on to name the next of her grievances.

> *Two: She is still making us do whatever she wants. She gave me the farm to force me to love it, which I do not, and then she makes us come here every year to visit it. And to visit her.*
>
> *And I don't want to have to go to that creepy graveyard the day after my birthday! Is that supposed to be, like, fun? I'm sick of her!! I know she's dead. Does she have to rub it in???*

Dilly opened a cautious eye and gazed around her mother's room, waiting for lightning to strike.

But it didn't.

Dilly thought about that second entry on her list. Her mother *had* left her the farm, true, but only because Peter

Howell—attorney at law—advised her to do so. And Dilly's dad always told Dilly she could sell the place one day, but not until she was old enough to make a truly informed decision about the matter, as he put it.

And as for visiting her mom's grave each year before leaving New York to return home to California, well, that tradition was started by her father. It hadn't been her mom's bright idea. It wasn't as if she were sitting on a cloud somewhere, trying to figure out how to boss them around, Dilly chided herself.

Well, Dilly thought stubbornly, but that led her to entry number three on her list of why she was so mad at her mother.

Three: She left me just when I needed her the most.

"I was only six years old," Dilly whispered to the darkening room—and to her mother, wherever she was. "Six! Couldn't you have held on for just a few more years?"

Memories flooded Dilly's mind: Of being sent to school in seriously not-cute outfits that the other girls couldn't help giggling at, with her hair badly cut by her dad's barber; of having no one to tell when her one-time best friend Jackie started that whispering campaign against her in the fourth grade, because how could she make her father even sadder when he was already so unhappy?

Of not having anyone to go to her school's stupid mother-daughter teas with. Every March was ruined for Dilly, each spring its own separate nightmare as she waited for the date of the tea to pass.

And who was going to tell her how to get over this maybe-fight with Sasha, probably the best friend she would ever, ever have? Isn't that what moms were supposed to be for?

Who would she ask whether or not she was really in love, when the time came?

Who would adjust her veil on her wedding day?

Who would help her figure out names for her babies?

"Just a few more years," Dilly said, louder now. "Couldn't you have lasted that much longer, Mummie? *For me?*"

Chapter Twelve Tea at the Sagamore

It started raining again during the night and it was still coming down hard the next morning.

Peter Howell seemed depressed at breakfast, and Dilly found herself suddenly wondering why. Maybe it was just the weather; Dilly wasn't feeling too cheerful herself.

Of course, it was Thursday, which meant Sasha would arrive tomorrow. That could have something to do with her mood.

Dilly trudged up the stairs after breakfast and flopped down onto her bed. Flat on her back, she found herself thinking about her mother—and about mothers in general. What would it be like, having one? Would she and her mom be best friends now if Elspeth Howell had lived?

Probably not, Dilly answered herself silently. Her friends at home didn't have that kind of relationship with their moms, and Sasha certainly didn't, either.

Sasha. Just how angry was her friend about her impending trip to Lake Luzerne? And did Sasha really blame her, Dilly, for having been made to come?

The uncomfortable tickle in Dilly's stomach told her how nervous she was at the prospect of seeing her friend again— if Sasha was going to act all miffed and everything.

Because a miffed Sasha was no fun, and that was putting things mildly.

Sasha was always complaining about *her* mother's unreasonable expectations about grades, and appearance, and "deportment," as Sasha claimed that her mom called it.

"Never touch your face or hair after you've left the privacy of the bathroom," Mrs. Thorne was supposed to have advised her daughter. And, *"Study hard now, young lady, because you are making the bed that you'll be lying in for the rest of your life."*

Stuff like that.

Still, Dilly thought, dragging her outspread arms back and forth across her bedspread, it might not be so horrible to have someone to tell you things. You could always ignore her, if she got on your nerves too much.

"My mom's always *telling* me stuff," she said aloud in a complaining voice, trying out the words.

Actually, Dilly admitted silently, those words sounded kind of cool.

"Let's run away for the afternoon," her father said as Dilly trudged down the stairs at lunchtime. He had been lying on the sofa, reading the *Post Star*—from cover to cover, it looked like. Sheets of newspaper littered the floor around him as if the storm outside had suddenly swept through the living room.

"Why?" Dilly asked teasingly. "Are you afraid if I get too bored, I'll turn into a troubled teen?"

It was one of their private, all-purpose jokes. When one of the little kids on their Pasadena street misbehaved in some small way, such as leaving a scooter in the driveway, Dilly might say, "Uh-oh—she'll probably grow up to be a troubled teen." When they watched the news and some grown-up villain's face flashed onto their TV screen, Peter Howell would observe, "I'll bet that guy used to be a troubled teen."

The joke proved useful at times, however. Whenever Dilly felt that she really, really needed to be alone, she only had to shout, "Future troubled teen coming through!" before she dashed into her room, and she knew her dad would give her as much privacy as she needed.

That's the way they were together, most of the time: quiet and comfortable. Peter Howell liked to read at night; seafaring adventures by Patrick O'Brian, lately. The Howells' one TV was in Dilly's bedroom, and she liked to watch it sometimes, but mostly when friends were over. Alone, she preferred to listen to CDs—with headphones on, because she considered her music private.

They often went out to dinner, but sometimes the housekeeper left a casserole for Dilly to stick in the oven at six o'clock. Other times, Dilly and her dad simply broiled a steak

or some salmon, popped baking potatoes into the micro-
wave, ripped open a bag of already-washed salad, and settled in to enjoy their evening meal together.

They didn't need anyone else, Dilly often told herself. They
were just fine.

Weekends, they usually stayed at home while Dilly worked
on projects for school or slept over at a friend's house.
Sometimes they went away for the weekend: Corona del Mar,
Big Bear, San Diego. Spring breaks were spent camping in
Anza-Borrego, which was a three-hour drive away. Wild-
flowers often carpeted the desert floor then with *Wizard of
Oz*–like abandon, and the encircling mountains—treeless,
and ribbed with rock, but hiding oases and small scrambling
herds of bighorn sheep—made Dilly's heart soar.

Other people hated the desert, thinking it empty and
harsh, but its very barrenness suited Dilly and her father perfectly. They found it beautiful—in March or April, anyway.

The desert was the complete opposite of Lake Luzerne,
Dilly thought, looking out of the living room window. "But how
can we run away? It's still raining," she said. "And there's
nothing to do around here. Where could we go? It's not like at
home, where it never rains in the summer and we can always
hike up to Henniger Flats."

"We'll go the Sagamore Hotel for tea," her dad said, as if
he were an amateur magician who had just successfully
pulled a rabbit from his hat. "With Sasha coming up tomor-

row, this'll be the last time I'll get to have you all to myself."

Maybe not, Dilly replied silently. *It depends on whether or not she's even speaking to me.*

She was excited about visiting the Sagamore, though, in spite of the fact that her mother had loved the luxurious old resort.

But Peter Howell didn't mention his wife, for once. "Tea at the Sagamore is exactly what you and I need today, Dilly-dill," he said. He swung his legs off the sofa and planted them firmly on the floor, as if he were following instructions in an invisible manual telling him how to look energetic.

"We'll have to get dressed up," Dilly reminded him.

"I can manage that," her dad said, grinning. "What about you?"

"Just watch me!"

Because of the rain, and because it was a Thursday, route 9N was relatively uncrowded. This was the sole road leading east through eight miles of forest from Lake Luzerne to the Northway, the wide highway Dilly and her dad took to and from the Albany airport each summer. The Northway ran all the way from Albany up to Canada.

This Sunday, however, Dilly and Peter Howell drove past the entrance to the Northway, having decided to continue following the curve of 9N north, taking the lake shore route. They passed Fort William Henry, then entered the village of

Lake George at the south end of the lake. T-shirted tourists milled up and down the gleaming sidewalks between cloud-bursts, determined to make the most of their vacations.

It was crowded in the village, but after Dilly and her father had inched their way through town, traffic thinned and Dilly settled back to enjoy the ride. She liked trying to catch glimpses through hedges and fake-rustic walls of the sprawl-ing lakeside houses that remained; their nineteenth-century owners had probably called these huge places "camps," in the style both of the day and of the region, Dilly remembered.

Even Snob Hill had been referred to as a camp at times, Dilly knew, as had many much more lavish, tycoon-built wa-terfront mansions tucked away on various rocky Adirondack shores.

Lazily, dreamily, she wished that rich old Ira Dillon, her great-great-grandfather, had built a fabulous place on a lake in 1889 rather than buying the farm from the Thornes. That would have been so cool! But no, he wanted land and privacy, and later on, Granny Tat wanted trees. So the Dillons had stayed on at Snob Hill.

And now it was all hers.

Hoo-ray.

"You're quiet," Peter Howell said, fiddling with the wind-shield wiper knob.

Dilly sneaked a sideways glance at her father. He looked especially handsome this afternoon, dressed in his light weight tweed jacket, khakis, vivid blue shirt, and tie. He'd somehow managed to get some sun during the past week, and his hair even looked a little bit lighter.

Her dad still seemed sad, though—or maybe he was just tired. "Did you sleep okay?" Dilly asked him, feeling like an actress in a play. She adjusted the snug cherry-patterned dress she'd brought with her to wear on special occasions. The print was retro in style, but it had been screened onto vivid chartreuse cotton that made your eyeballs jump when you looked at it.

"Yeah, I slept fine. What about you?"

Dilly adjusted the vent. "Fine," she said. They were silent for a couple of minutes. Peter Howell sighed, then he swerved the car slightly to avoid a rain-sodden bough that had fallen onto the road.

"We're at Bolton Landing," Dilly remarked, just for something to say, and her father slowed down for the crawl through that village.

They began looking for the turn-off to the Sagamore.

The old hotel section of the resort was sparkling white in the rain. Built in a gentle curve facing the water, the building's wide arms seemed to embrace colorfully planted terraces that stepped gradually down to Lake George. Dilly and her dad darted across the parking lot behind the hotel, then paused at the rear-facing entry to rid themselves of their wet umbrellas.

Inside, the Sagamore seemed more like a club than it did a hotel; people were a little dressed up, at least by Lake Luzerne summer standards. But there was a relaxed feeling to the place, as though in spite of the rain, people had decided to make the best of things. And why not, in such surroundings?

Dilly tugged a little at her dress, however, wishing now that it were just a little bit longer. "Don't worry," her dad murmured. "You're the prettiest girl here. You brighten up a gray day."

She flashed him a grateful smile.

Instead of sitting in the dining room, they decided to have their tea in the wide bright room overlooking the water. More was going on there.

Determined au pairs rustled little clusters of children into their yellow slickers and out the terrace door, despite the weather. Sporty old ladies who looked as though they'd much rather be out bird-watching on a nearby mountainside sat down, crossed their elegant ankles, and made do with martinis or glasses of chilled white wine. Men and women who Dilly secretly hoped were honeymooning couples leaned their heads together in earnest conversation, occasionally feeding each other a strawberry or a chocolate-dipped piece of shortbread.

Their waiter snapped open Dilly's crisp white napkin with a flourish and placed it delicately across her lap, as if he were presenting her with a welcoming bouquet. "This is where I proposed to your mother," Dilly's dad said, after selecting a tea for them and settling back into his creaky wicker chair.

"Right here?" Dilly asked, looking around the room with renewed interest.

"Well, actually it was on one of those benches outside," Peter Howell admitted, laughing at his daughter's passion for detail. "It was an absolutely brilliant autumn day. I'll never forget it—even though it was nearly twenty years ago. I'd been invited to stay at the farm for a lo-o-ng weekend, and Elle and I made our getaway one afternoon when things got to be just a little too much for us there."

The waiter brought a pot of tea to their table and then arranged a plate of crustless sandwiches and a tiered display of long-stemmed strawberries, tiny iced cakes, and sugar-dusted cookies between them. "Yum," Dilly said, her eyes wide as she looked at everything on the table.

"Yum," her dad agreed happily, and they helped themselves from the tempting assortment of food. After a couple of minutes, Dilly poured their tea.

"Elspeth told me once that when she was a very little girl, she used to put milk and sugar in her tea," Peter Howell said, "never lemon."

"I'm going to try having mine that way," Dilly announced shyly, and she watched fascinated as a trickle of milk made a crazy swirl in the clear hot tea. "Did Granny Tat think you were good enough to marry Mummie?" she asked, transferring an amber lump of sugar by spoon from its silver bowl into her cup. She avoided looking at her father as she asked this awkward question.

"Eventually," Peter Howell said, smiling at the memory. "But I sure had to prove myself to her. Slay a few dragons, and so on. It was a two-year engagement. Why do you ask?"

Dilly busily stirred her tea. "I don't know. You did tell me that she was kind of a snob."

Her father laughed out loud. "*Kind of* a snob? Gee, Dilly— don't go out on a limb or anything! But I know what you're try- ing to say, and the answer is basically yes, Granny Tat thought I was a good enough match for your mother. Not that any ob- jection of hers could have slowed Elspeth or me down. Elle had a lot of gumption—more than enough to stand up to your Granny Tat, believe me."

"That's good," Dilly said, nibbling at a strawberry.

"Of course, your great-grandmother didn't like it one bit when Elle and I moved to California, but by then it was too late. We were already married."

"Why, what was wrong with California?" Dilly asked, feel- ing instantly resentful on behalf of the entire state.

"Wrong coast," her father said succinctly. "Granny Tat just never could take the place seriously. Of course the real rea- son she didn't want us to move was because it meant she'd be losing Elspeth—during the winters, anyway, although Elle always managed to get back to Boston for a week or two each spring. That went on for seven years, until Granny Tat died. Well, you probably remember making a couple of those trips with Mummie, don't you?"

"Not really," Dilly admitted, although all at once she did

recall some shiny marble stairs, a secluded, curtain-enclosed window seat, and a very old lady with loving blue eyes who swept her into a bony hug that made Dilly feel as if she were being folded up inside a Japanese fan. Like the one her mother used to let her play with sometimes in Pasadena, now that she thought about it.

"No, Granny Tat and I got along all right," Peter Howell said, pouring out some more tea. "In fact, I really came to like the old girl. That's one of the reasons I'm thankful she never knew what was in store for your mother. Poor old Granny Tat thought everything was all settled. Elspeth would inherit the farm, and we'd keep returning each year to the correct coast—for the summers, at least. And things would go on as they always had, and the three of us would all live happily ever after."

"But instead, Mummie died and I ended up with the farm," Dilly said, placing a half-eaten sandwich back on her plate.

"That's right. And I guess you and I are living happily ever after."

Dilly hesitated for a moment. "Is it really mine, Daddy?" she asked her father.

"Of course it is. You know that."

"But I mean, what if I actually do decide that I want to sell it?"

"Then you'll sell it. But not until you're grown, Dilly."

"How old is 'grown'?" Dilly asked, leaning forward in her chair. "Eighteen? Twenty-one?"

Dilly's father looked at her, frowning slightly now. "Do you really hate it all that much, honey?" he finally asked.

"Oh, I don't know," Dilly finally said to her father, looking away. "I just don't like feeling trapped, that's all."

"But you're not trapped," her father replied mildly, helping himself to another cucumber and cream cheese sandwich. "What makes you think you're trapped?"

"Well, we do the exact same thing every year, don't we? Just because Mummie wanted us to?" Dilly asked, frustration making her bold.

Peter Howell gazed out at the rain-pocked lake. The uneaten sandwich drooped in his hand. "You know," he finally said, "I don't think she ever *said* what she wanted us to do—about visiting the farm, I mean. She probably just assumed we would love it the way she always had, and that we'd *want* to come."

"Do you?" Dilly asked her father.

"I—I guess I never thought about it all that much," her dad admitted. "I do like it a lot. And coming here is something we've always done. So we keep on doing it."

"We're stuck," Dilly concluded. And stuck was the same as trapped.

Just the way she was trapped being mad at her mom, she thought, surprised. "Listen," she said softly, urgently. "I want to hear the *bad* stuff about Mummie."

Peter Howell scowled, his mouth now full. "The bad stuff?"

he finally repeated. "But there wasn't any bad stuff, Dilly. Elspeth was—"

"Perfect," Dilly said bitterly, finishing the sentence for him. "I know. And now that she's dead, she just keeps getting more and more perfect every year, doesn't she? Well, don't you think that's kind of a hard thing for me to live up to?"

The Sagamore itself seemed to hold its breath while Dilly's father digested this outburst. "I suppose so," he finally said, obviously struggling to keep his voice mild. "Maybe it's too hard for anyone to live up to."

"Wasn't Mummie sometimes unreasonable about things?" Dilly asked, feeling guilty and frustrated at the same time. "Didn't she ever look like a slob, at least every so often? Don't you think she ever got *mad* about anything?" she continued before she could lose her nerve. Her heart was hammering in her chest, however; she was surprised that you couldn't see the front of her dress bounce with each emphatic beat.

"She sure did," her father said, obviously trying to collect his thoughts. "She could be kind of a handful at times, as a matter of fact. Moody, and so on. Used to having her own way, too—well, Granny Tat had spoiled her some. And she didn't like it one little bit when I had to stay late at the office. And she absolutely *hated* being sick. It made her furious, at least at first. She drove me nuts, then—I didn't know what to say to her, or how to act. There was no pleasing her."

It all came out in a rush.

Dilly blinked, startled at this onslaught of information.

"How come you never told me any of this before?" she asked her father.

Peter Howell buried his head in his hands at this last question. "Oh, baby, I don't know," he said, his voice muffled. "You were so little when she died. And I guess I wanted you to remember just the good things about Elle."

"But I barely remember *anything* about her! Not really," Dilly said, trying to keep her voice down.

Her father looked up at her, stricken. "I don't either," he finally replied, and to Dilly's horror, his brown eyes filled with tears.

"Oh, Daddy," she said, instantly remorseful, and she sneaked a peek at the surrounding tables. Her father absolutely never cried—even in private. And she had brought these tears to his eyes! "That's okay," she said, trying to reach across the table to pat his shoulder.

"No, it's *not* okay," he said, running his hands back through his hair as he collected himself. "When Elspeth got her final diagnosis, I promised her that I would never forget one minute of our lives together. But now, I can barely picture her face, not without looking at a photograph. And it's only been six years since she died!"

"Six years is a long time, Daddy. It's half of my entire life."

Dilly's father shook his head. "But six years is just one-seventh of my life," he pointed out. "Maybe that's why it seems to me as though it just happened."

Dilly did some quick figuring. One-seventh of *her* life

would be—well, little more than a year and a half. And a year and a half after her mother died, she was still stumbling around like a miniature zombie. No wonder six years seemed like a short time to her dad!

"I can't picture her face either," Dilly told him, her voice soft. "I—I'm sorry I made you say all those bad things about Mummie."

"I'm not," her father replied, laughing a little shakily. "It brought her back to me for a moment."

"Do you still miss her, Daddy?"

Peter Howell was quiet for almost a full tick-tocking minute, and Dilly imagined that she could hear his heart beating. "I used to miss her all the time," he finally said softly, as if confessing something. "Now, I'm just lonely, I guess—to be perfectly honest. Even though you and I still have each other, Dilly."

In a way, Dilly felt hurt, hearing these words. Shouldn't her dad be in love with her mom for all eternity? And shouldn't having her, Dilly, to love here on earth be enough to keep him from being lonely, at least?

But on the other hand, she understood what her father meant. Sort of. Because she was lonely, too.

She was glad he'd said it, anyway—because it sounded like the truth. And that's what she'd asked for, wasn't it?

Chapter Thirteen  Extremely Urban Sasha

Peter Howell was carrying sacks of groceries in from the car early Friday afternoon just as Dilly plodded up the driveway, tired from her solitary walk down to the river. "You made it just in time," he said, gesturing up at the sky, which was darkening fast as storm clouds seemed to tumble over the rounded mountains behind the river. "Here, can you take this?" he added, handing Dilly a bag.

"Why did you buy all this food?" Dilly asked. They had planned to go into town for dinner that night.

"Well," her father said, "I bumped into Libby at the library, and—"

Libby! "You didn't *say* you were going to the library," Dilly interrupted accusingly, plunking her grocery bag onto the kitchen table just as the first crack of thunder echoed around them. Now, she was afraid to look at her dad. What had Libby told him?

Dilly's father was baffled by her outburst. "It was kind of a spur-of-the-moment thing, Dilly. We can go back to the library tomorrow if you need to check out something to read."

"It's not that," Dilly mumbled, taking things out of the grocery bag.

A sack of rice. Broccoli. Four shiny cellophane-wrapped packets of lamb chops. "Lamb chops?" Dilly asked. "I thought we were going out to the Waterhouse."

"Well, but now we're having company," her father explained, looking pleased. "See, I got to talking with Libby in the library. She even made us up a pot of coffee in that little office she has in the back. And—long story short—Libby and Sasha are coming over for dinner tonight. Surprise!"

Dilly merely blinked at him.

"Libby's picking Sasha up in Saratoga Springs at about five o'clock," Dilly's father was saying. "I offered to go get her instead, because of the storm and everything, but Libby said she wanted a chance for them to have a nice private talk."

I'll just bet, Dilly thought.

"But that's good, actually," Peter Howell said, fishing a yellowed old cookbook down from the shelf. "Because I'm going to make a pie out of those blueberries I picked this morning. Want to help? We can get started right away," he said, as if pie-baking might be a task that would take hours and hours.

He was totally *up* for this dinner party, Dilly realized angrily just as the rain started to fall once more. But at least he wasn't yelling at her about being rude to Libby.

Libby must have decided to keep her mouth shut.

"Sorry, I've got plans," Dilly said, trying not to snap out the words.

"Well, okay. But I'm going to want you to set the table after I finish assembling this pie," her father said, holding up a wooden spoon as if he were a conductor raising his baton.

"Don't I always?" Dilly muttered, but not loudly enough for her dad to hear.

After all, she thought bitterly, there was no point in pressing her luck.

In spite of everything, Dilly's mouth watered that afternoon as the aroma of baking pie filled the house. She swallowed hard and jerked open another bureau drawer in the upstairs guest room. One of the drawer's glass knobs wiggled in her hand as if it might come off. "Perfect. That's all I need," Dilly grumbled under her breath as she looked around the darkened room, lit only by two bedside lamps.

The guest room was papered in a dark blue pattern that had probably seemed to be a good idea at the time, Dilly thought wryly. The result was what a decorator might call old-fashioned and snug, but to Dilly, the room looked just plain gloomy. Of course, the rainy afternoon wasn't helping much.

This had been Granny Tat's room once, Dilly remembered being told.

Dilly patted her hand across the shadowy bottom of the drawer to see if there was something there. Two pennies, a nickel, and a safety pin were the result of this search. "I'm rich beyond my wildest dreams," Dilly said mockingly to herself, but she pocketed the coins.

Downstairs, her dad was singing "On the Road Again," and something clattered to the floor. "Don't worry, everything's fine!" he called up the stairs. Dilly couldn't help but giggle.

Just then, a double crash of thunder made the guest room's two paltry lights flicker, and a big hexagonal soup tureen on top of the bureau rattled on its matching platter. Dilly put a hand out to steady it.

Like many such objects at the farm, this tureen seemed always to have lived where it now was, although Dilly couldn't imagine why anyone would want to ladle out soup in a bedroom. Possibly—much more likely, in fact—the tureen had served as a container for years-gone flower arrangements.

Dilly could picture gold daylilies, vivid blue chicory flowers, and a white froth of Queen Anne's lace overflowing its wide opening, which was now neatly covered with a lid whose handle was several twists of porcelain fashioned to resemble entwined grape vines. A matching porcelain spoon poked out of a hole at the side of the lid.

Suddenly, impulsively, Dilly lifted the lid from the tureen.

A couple of hours later, Dilly fidgeted with her dinner napkin and tried to avoid an extremely urban Sasha Thorne's questioning glances. Dinner was just about over, and Libby hadn't said a word about their fight all evening, thank goodness.

It was almost a year since Dilly and Sasha had last seen each other. Sasha hadn't grown much—she was still just a little over five feet two inches tall, while Dilly was almost four inches taller—but Sasha had honed her style over the past year. Instead of the bedraggled, below-the-shoulder hairstyle that had always reminded Dilly of the little girl called Wednesday in the Addams Family movies, Sasha's glossy black hair was now much shorter and sleeker. This new style made her look all the more Sasha-like, Dilly thought: hip and ironic. Her clothes were cooler than ever, too.

But then, Sasha had never dressed much differently in Lake Luzerne than she did at home in the city. "Yeah, right— like *that's* gonna happen!" she always said, laughing, whenever Dilly offered her a dusty windbreaker or faded jacket from the selection hanging in the pantry. She would rather freeze, thanks.

Peter Howell did not appear to notice that there was any awkwardness between Dilly and Libby—or Dilly and Sasha, for that matter—during dinner. He was too busy being both host and cook. His brown hair was tousled in a most un-lawyerlike way, and he sported a blue-and-white striped dish towel draped over one shoulder all throughout dinner.

He was also busy being charming to Libby, Dilly couldn't help but notice; he had touched her arm twice, blushing the second time. The two grown-ups were babbling on and on about the Napoleonic wars, which was what all of Patrick O'Brian's books were about, apparently. Libby had read them too. *Great,* Dilly thought, brooding.

Black-and-gray-clad Sasha seemed oblivious to the possibility that anything unusual was happening between her aunt and Dilly's father. She did appear to notice some disturbance between Dilly and Libby, but its source was obviously a mystery to her. She scowled pensively throughout much of dinner, but that wasn't so unusual.

Dilly's father helped Libby to more broccoli. "I saw a flock of wild turkeys down in the field this morning," he said proudly, as if he himself had invited them there.

"Lucky you," Libby said, pushing with her fork at the mound of rice he'd served her earlier. "I love the way they scurry along, with their round backs—sort of like a little herd of armadillos, I always think."

Peter Howell beamed his approval of this whimsical remark, and Sasha rolled her eyes, then turned her head to make a hidden gagging motion, forefinger on tongue.

Only Dilly saw her do this. For the first time that evening, she felt like laughing.

"No more rice, thanks, Peter," Libby told Dilly's father. "I've had enough."

Haven't we all, Dilly replied silently, savagely.

❖   ❖   ❖

When at long last it was time for dessert, Peter Howell's blueberry pie was passed triumphantly around the kitchen table, and Sasha slid a large slab onto her plate. Since she had announced moments before dinner that she no longer ate meat—and even if she still ate meat, it wouldn't be *lamb chops*—she was still hungry, following her spartan meal of plain white rice and a single stalk of broccoli.

"I'm glad to see that vegetarians can eat pie," Libby remarked, topping her own modest slice with some vanilla ice cream as she smiled her thanks at Dilly's dad.

"As long as it's not *lamb* pie," Sasha said, unperturbed. She took an enormous bite. "Or spare rib pie. Or fried chicken pie. But I told you all the stuff I could and couldn't eat, Aunt Libby. Remember? In that letter I sent you?"

Another letter. Just what this nightmare of a dinner party needed, Dilly thought. She moved her own piece of pie around her dessert plate, suddenly too jangled to eat it. She sneaked a peek at Libby, but Libby appeared simply to be enjoying her dessert. "Eat up, Dilly-dill," her father told her playfully. "You've got some dishes to do."

For once, Dilly found that she was almost looking forward to this nightly chore. At least then, she'd get to be alone.

"And Sasha will help," Libby said, volunteering her niece's services.

"Why doesn't Sasha just sleep over tonight?" Peter Howell suggested. "We can always find a spare toothbrush, and I'm sure Dilly has an extra nightgown Sasha can borrow."

Since Sasha was probably mad at her for being dragged up to Lake Luzerne, and since her irked friend usually slept only in a big old T-shirt from some rock concert or other, Dilly didn't think either of her dad's suggestions would go over too well. But to her surprise, Sasha merely shrugged. "Okay," she said. "As long as I can sleep late."

So that was settled. But it wasn't so much a case of Sasha *wanting* to sleep over, Dilly realized. Rather, Sasha didn't really care where she slept, if she didn't get to sleep at home in the city.

That was it, Dilly thought: The good old days were officially over.

Chapter Fourteen  Homesike for You

Because of the nearby Adirondacks and the hill that loomed behind the Howells' old farmhouse, the television in the Howells' living room only got one channel, and cable TV had yet to come to Riverview Road, so—after Libby had announced she was going to make an early night of it and go home—the girls went right upstairs when the dishes were done so that they could listen to music.

"I've always really loved this wallpaper," Sasha said, stifling a yawn and not even looking around as she walked into Dilly's bedroom. "Except I've gotta tell you, it kind of looks like Laura Ashley exploded in here."

"She did," Dilly drawled, trying to sound just as bored as Sasha. "The forensics team left just as you and Libby were pulling up. I'm surprised you didn't see the big black van with the skull and crossbones on the side."

Sasha grinned, then ran her hand back through her shiny hair and gave a dramatic sigh. "It is so *quiet* up here in the country," she said—exactly the way someone else would complain about a jackhammer pounding the street outside.

"Just wait until the local whippoorwill starts yelling his

head off," Dilly said. "You'll be begging for a little peace and quiet, then, Sash."

"I forgot all about whippoorwills," Sasha said. "Hey, what's this?" she asked idly, reaching for a lavender ribbon-wrapped stack of papers on Dilly's bureau.

Dilly grabbed for the papers, but it was too late.

"What's *this*?" Sasha asked again, teasing now.

"Just some stuff I found stashed away in my Granny Tat's room," Dilly mumbled, thinking fast. "Inside an old soup tureen." There was no harm in letting Sasha see what she'd found, Dilly told herself. It was only a few letters, after all—letters that she herself had written.

A long time ago.

"Go ahead and read them, if you want to," Dilly said to Sasha, shrugging. "I don't care."

December 18, 1993

Dear Santa Claus,

I would like a nice baby doll, a new twirly dress, doll silverware, and a small dollhouse. I tried to be a good girl.

Thank you very much.

Dilly

Sasha looked up from the old letter with a look of mock horror on her face. "Jeepers," she said in the pretend old-fashioned tone she sometimes affected. "Did you really write this thing?" She sat down on Dilly's bed with the letters and pulled an old patchwork quilt up over her legs.

Dilly laughed. "I dictated it, anyway. That's my mother's writing," she said, trying to sound as if this were no big deal.

Sasha peered at the letter once more, and a lock of shiny black hair flopped over her brow. "You certainly were a domestic little squirt," she observed wryly. "Silverware? And a *small* dollhouse? Why didn't you ask for a mansion, as long as you were going to chain yourself down in suburbia like that?" She shook her head, pretending to be appalled. "*'Twirly dress,'*" she muttered.

Dilly had started laughing, in spite of everything. In fact, she was laughing so hard that she could barely answer— partly because Sasha was being funny, and partly for some other reason that she could not really identify. Relief, per- haps—that Sasha was finally loosening up a little. Maybe these were *still* the good old days.

The mental image she suddenly had was of an old black- and-white photograph she'd seen once on the wall at the Lake Luzerne Historical Society. At least one hundred years old, the picture showed the upper Hudson River completely jammed with logs. The small upright loggers balancing on the logs in the photograph had just broken up the jam with long poles, and one or two of the logs were shooting off downstream.

"I—I was only three that Christmas," Dilly finally managed to say to Sasha. "Give me a break."

Sasha shook her head again and turned to the photograph that had been clipped to this first letter. In the picture, a pudgy but recognizable little Dilly was sitting on Santa's lap. "Now, this is just plain sick," Sasha said, as if she were an archaeologist who had just unearthed proof of a particularly bizarre ancient practice. "Santa looks like he's bombed out of his mind in this picture, and you look absolutely terrified, like you're about to wet your pants. Some treat this was! And what's with the long number at the bottom of the picture?" she continued, jabbing an accusatory finger. "It makes this look like a prison mug shot. *'Officer! Arrest that little girl!'* "

Dilly wiped tears of laughter from her eyes as a gust of wind shook her window in its frame. The curtains seemed to shiver for a moment. "Don't try to tell me that your mom never made you do this when you were a kid," she said. "Like at that great big Macy's?"

"Well, she might have," Sasha admitted grudgingly. "But I would have asked Santa for something good, like real estate, maybe. And I would never have said that I *tried* to be a good girl. I would have flat-out lied about it."

"Wait—this letter's not quite as bad," Dilly said, pulling another letter from the small pile of papers.

> *December 23, 1994*
>
> *Dear Santa,*
>   *Hi! I would like a toy elephant. I also want some crayons and a blackboard and a book that I can read.*
>
> > *Your friend,*
> > *Dilly Howell*

" 'Your friend,' " Sasha repeated aloud. "You were getting to be kind of a kiss-up by then, weren't you?"

"I guess," Dilly giggled. "But note the request for the book. I was getting smarter, anyway."

"Except for waiting until December twenty-third to write the letter," Sasha pointed out, peering at the date. "You've got to give the old guy plenty of notice," she added wisely. "That way, there can be no excuse for him not coming through. Where's the mug shot?"

"No picture that year, I guess," Dilly said, shuffling through the papers.

"I guess you wised up," Sasha said. "You probably told your parents, 'How come you go through the whole year telling me not to talk to strangers, and then you order me to sit on that man's lap? They don't get any stranger than him!' I like the 'Hi,' though. Very jaunty. Just the right note."

"Here's another one," Dilly said, handing Sasha the letter.

November 32, 1995
Dear Santa Claus . . .
> *I want . . . a . . . sleepy bag . . . and some new vidos . . . and a doll . . . and some good books. Also, I should like some new socks . . .*
>> *Your friend . . .*
>> *Dilly Howell*

"November thirty-second?" Sasha squawked. "Where were you living, in the Twilight Zone? And what's with all the dots?"

"Well, see, I wrote that letter myself," Dilly tried to explain while stifling her laughter. "I guess I must have seen dots like that in a book and liked the way they looked."

"If you say so," Sasha said skeptically. "But what's a sleepy bag?"

"Sleeping bag," Dilly interpreted, and a memory of soft red-and-green plaid flannel lining came back to her. "And 'vidos' are videos," she continued. "I used to watch a lot of TV back then," she added. She didn't say why, however. But Dilly was surprised to feel a sudden flicker of loneliness somewhere just behind her throat.

"Well, I can buy all that," Sasha was saying. "But, *'I should like some new socks'*? What's *that* about? You sound like you're channeling the Queen of England!"

Dilly shook her head and smiled once more, not able to answer the question. "Maybe I'd been watching some old movie where they talked like that," she guessed. "I must have had to ask how to spell 'should,' that's for sure. I *still* have to think about it at times."

"Any more Christmas letters?" Sasha asked, looking hopefully at the papers that were left. "What about 1996?"

And then she remembered: Elspeth Howell had died in the summer of 1996, and she was obviously the one who had been saving Dilly's letters.

"That's okay, Sasha," Dilly said, seeing the look on her friend's face. "There's some other stuff here," she added, as if hoping to make Sasha feel better about having made such a mistake.

"Like what?"

"There are some notes I must have written to my mother," Dilly said, pulling out a few scraps of paper. "They're pretty good."

I love you! Tuck me in wehn you get home!
Love, Dilly!

"Short and sweet," Sasha said approvingly. "Kind of overexcited, though. My English teacher says that you should only use an exclamation mark if your keyboard is on fire."

Dilly laughed. "This one's a little more serious," she said, passing the next note to Sasha.

YOU LOOK LIKE THIS. I HAT YOU.
Love, Dilly.

A drawing was attached to this message with a paper clip. It depicted an animal that had been drawn in black marker lines so bold and angry that they had torn the paper in places.

"Is that supposed to be an elephant?" Sasha asked, squinting at the drawing.

"I guess so," Dilly said, laughing. "Big ears, long trunk."

"So, we return to the pachyderm motif," Sasha said with a scholarly air. "You know, repeating your earlier gift request. This one's got a nasty expression on its face, though," Sasha added. "I assume you were saying you hated her, not that you hatted her."

"I guess," Dilly said again. She shook her head, bemused. "But I can't remember why I was so mad at my mother. What could she have done?"

"You probably had your reasons," Sasha told her, loyal to that long-gone, five-year-old child.

Dilly flushed with gratitude, though she tried to hide it. "This is the last one," she said.

> *I love you.*
> *I miss you.*
> *I em homesike for you.*
>
> > *Love, Dilly*

" 'I am homesick for you,' " Dilly said softly, before Sasha could even ask.

"Now, that's just plain sad," Sasha said, not joking for once. "I think I'm about to start crying—like a big old baby."

Dilly was even more moved than before, hearing Sasha say this. The fact that these letters and notes had been so carefully saved was, after all, physical evidence of how much her mother had loved her, Dilly realized. Here too was proof of how close she and her mom had once been.

And Sasha was witness, moved almost to tears by Dilly's childhood scribblings.

But to her astonishment—and horror—she realized that

she, Dilly, was the one with tears streaming down her face.

"I—I have to tell you something," she told Sasha between gulping sobs. "You're not going to believe what my mother did just before she died. . . ."

Chapter Fifteen Fight!

The girls were up until almost 2:30 A.M. talking about the still-unfound letter Dilly's mom had written. Sasha thought they should just find it, read it, and then toss it, if Dilly still wanted to. Get the whole thing over with—*fast.*

"But I know you, Dilly," she said, resigned. "You're just like one of those crazy birds who builds her nest in a traffic light. Then you spend the rest of the summer wondering, *'Why me? Why me? Why me?'* every time the light changes."

"What's that supposed to mean?" Dilly asked, highly offended.

But Sasha did know her, she admitted to herself. And she knew Sasha. Hadn't they been stranded together for twelve summers on Riverview Road, several miles away from even the tiny town of Lake Luzerne?

There was more to their friendship than mere isolation, however. Only Dilly knew how Sasha still chewed at the side of her forefinger at night when she was trying to fall asleep. Only Dilly knew that Sasha secretly fretted that one of her legs was shorter than the other. Only Dilly knew how worried

Sasha already was about getting into the kind of college that would satisfy her mother and father.

And only Sasha knew about the bad dreams that sometimes caused Dilly to awaken with a stifled cry when she was at the farm, her heart pounding with loneliness. Awkward but tender, Sasha would jostle her friend until she was fully awake and then listen attentively while Dilly talked about her dream in a hurried whisper.

And the next day, Sasha never mentioned what had happened.

"What's that supposed to mean?" Dilly asked again, more gently this time.

"It means that I think you're just looking for something to be mad about. It means you pick the dumbest little thing to get all worked up over in the first place, and then you keep on staying mad about it. I don't happen to think it's good for you, Dilly. But it gives you something to do, I guess."

"That is so offensive," Dilly said, almost sputtering with indignation. "And this is not a dumb little thing!"

"Okay, okay—have it your way," Sasha said soothingly. "It's the *perfect* thing to drive yourself nuts over. But if you insist on looking for the letter, you can put me in charge of searching Libby's house," she told Dilly. "But in return, you have to promise me that you'll take a break from this whole letter thing, all right? Because I'm worried about you, Dilly! So will you at least give it a rest for a while—you *obsessive nut*? Since you can't find the letter anyway?"

"Well . . ."

"Do we have a deal, or don't we?"

"Deal," Dilly agreed reluctantly.

Late the next morning, Dilly's father announced that he was going into the village. "The bank, the hardware store, the gas station," he said, listing his planned stops. "Do you girls want to come?"

"That's pretty tempting, but no thanks," Dilly said, laughing, as she exchanged a sardonic glance with Sasha, who was buttering a piece of rye toast.

"What are you going to do today? Not more sorting, I hope," her dad said, washing his hands at the sink.

"No sorting today, Dad," Dilly told her father, after exchanging a quick look with Sasha. "I think we'll probably go for a walk in the woods, as long as the sun's out," she said, as Sasha nodded approvingly.

"Well, you two stay on the paths if you go into the forest," her father advised over his shoulder. "Remember, it's easy to get turned around up there."

"Don't worry, Daddy. *'I have a special relationship with nature,'*" Dilly said, rolling her eyes behind her father's back as she repeated an old, often-quoted boast of Granny Tat's that had been passed down in the family as if it were a silver teapot.

"Me too," Sasha chimed in. "My relationship with nature is

that I stay as far away from it as possible. *Usually.* But today, I'll make an exception."

Their walk would take the form of a giant, if uneven, figure eight. The first loop was to be the small one, through the field opposite the house. Then Dilly and Sasha would head up into the forest behind the house and eventually curve around back down to Riverview Road.

Dilly dressed in layers in case it got hot and she needed to take a sweater off, and she even tucked a big folded-up trash sack in her hip pocket to cover her if it rained, causing Sasha to roll her eyes in horror. But Dilly figured she could poke holes in the bag for her head and arms, if necessary. It was easier than lugging along one of the stiff and smelly old slickers that was hanging in the pantry.

That was a good thing about the farm, Dilly told herself as she squeezed past the peeling, listing gate and let herself into the sunlit eight-acre field. You could do dumb stuff such as wearing a trash sack in the rain and never feel like an idiot, unless you looked at the expression on Sasha's face.

In Pasadena, you couldn't even walk out to the curb to get the newspaper in the morning without bumping into a couple of people. Wear a trash sack in Southern California, and a SWAT team would surround you before you could say how-do-you-do.

Here, however, your privacy was assured.

Dilly heard herself humming as she veered left across the field toward Libby Thorne's house. *Libby, Libby, Libby.* She hadn't *quite* gotten around to telling Sasha last night about her fight with Libby. Dilly could easily enough confess that she'd accused Libby of hiding the letter, she figured, but she didn't want to admit that she'd called Libby—Sasha's aunt!—pathetic.

There was no explaining that away.

And she couldn't show Sasha the letters that Elle and Libby had exchanged when Elle's parents had died, not without revealing how selfish and bossy her mom had been—*and* reminding Sasha of the spooky similarity of their present situation.

So she was stuck once more, basically, Dilly told herself. She could not ask Sasha why she thought her aunt had asked her up here without focusing Sasha's laserlike attention on *everything.* Once Sasha started digging, the whole embarrassing mess would be exposed—and then Sasha might be mad at her all over again.

And she could not risk that.

She definitely should call Libby up and apologize, and *soon,* Dilly lectured herself.

Behind her, Sasha swore under her breath—at an impudent twig, perhaps, or a hidden hole in the ground. "Stupid *field,*" she snarled.

"Keep up the good work, Sash," Dilly called back over her shoulder.

Libby. Dilly's father always told her that a mature person didn't need to be perfect, but he or she did have to know when to say, *"I'm sorry, I was wrong. Period,"* her father always added.

No excuses.

" 'Never complain, never explain.' That's what Mummie used to say," Peter Howell had told Dilly on more than one occasion.

Not that Dilly had anything to complain about in her relationship with Libby; Libby had never been anything but kind to her. And there wasn't really any explanation Dilly could think of for what she'd said to Libby: accusing her of wanting to tattle; implying that she was after Dilly's dad.

Why had she done that? Dilly berated herself. Would it be so terrible if her father were interested in Libby Thorne? Or interested in *anyone*?

Yes.

Peter Howell had been shattered after his wife's death; everyone said so. But he had quickly pulled himself together well enough to focus his attentions on three things: what Elspeth would have wanted, work, and Dilly.

And she had always liked being such an important part of her father's life, Dilly admitted to herself. Why mess with a good thing?

"Ow," Sasha complained, leaning over to rub her ankle. "I'll bet even your California friends Frecka and Bean couldn't take *this* walk, Dilly. It's like some crazy reality-TV episode."

Dilly giggled. "Becka and Fran," she corrected Sasha.

"And it's your extremely cool boots that are slowing you down."

"Bucky and Flan, then. And my boots are just perfect, thank you very much."

"We're only walking through a poky little field," Dilly continued. But she helped Sasha up onto an exposed piece of granite, and they surveyed the golden stubble around them. The entire field seemed to revolve—wheel-like—around a central massive birch tree that had been allowed to grow and thrive.

When she'd been little, Dilly remembered suddenly, she collected long white scraps of birch bark the tree had shed and pretended to read them. The sketchy black marks on the bark were really secret messages the deer wrote, Dilly told her mother.

Really, Dilly recalled, the idea that those birch bark markings could convey information hadn't seemed any more unlikely to her then than had the idea of reading other marks—letters, forming words—on a printed page.

Pat the Bunny. Pat the Bunny.

On other occasions, ever since she'd been old enough to cross Riverview Road without holding someone's hand, Dilly had fled to the birch tree's shelter when she simply needed to be alone.

Her mother had done that, too—when she was a girl, Dilly was told once by her father.

Well.

"I guess we can go on, now," Sasha said, not bothering to hide the yawn that followed.

Dilly and Sasha leapt off the rock and set off around the rest of the field with longer strides, the dried mown grass crunching under their feet. Stone walls surrounded three sides of the field, walls that had been built during the hundred and fifty years prior to the Civil War.

"Your ancestors built all these walls," Dilly told Sasha, looking around.

"Don't remind me," Sasha snapped. "I think I must have inherited their blisters."

Walking fast, in spite of Sasha's alleged blisters, they finished circling the field in just fifteen minutes. They crossed the road, and Sasha looked longingly toward the farmhouse. "Not yet," Dilly said, and they made their way up past the barn to the hill that led up to the woods.

"You're not the boss of me," Sasha grumbled, pretending to be a little kid again.

"Sure I am," Dilly joked, laughing. "You know that."

The hill just behind the barn was half given over to a treacherous tangle of blackberry bushes, but the narrow trail leading through them soon widened as the hill got steeper. This was the only part of the walk that had ever been at all strenuous when Dilly was a toddler.

She suddenly remembered holding on to her mother's

warm hand as they trudged up this very hill. How safe she had felt then!

The path was cushioned by a thick pad of pine needles as they climbed, Sasha's long black coat flapping around her calves. They finally reached the top, passing through an opening in yet another stone wall, one that had surrounded an additional pasture.

And the woods opened up before them.

Various paths had been worn through the forest over the years. Some of them were created by cattle, before most of the dairy farms had been closed down in the 1950s; some by generations of Thornes and Dillons; and some by the forester who was hired to come in every five years or so and harvest the trees ready to be cut down. The white pines and hemlocks towered above their heads, most of the trees as upright as telephone poles.

Here at the top of Snob Hill—roughly eighty acres of forest belonging to the farm, to Dilly—the land rose and dipped in places but was basically level. Dilly and Sasha worked their way slowly back toward the rear property line, which was at yet another stone wall, this one half buried now in fifty years' worth of pine needles. It was strange seeing the wild forest divided by these fallen walls, reminders of a more cultivated past—almost as if you had come upon an old rubber duckie floating in the middle of a stormy sea.

❖ ❖ ❖

The trees were crowded and tall at the rear of Dilly's property; perhaps they grew too far back for the forester to harvest profitably. Dilly and Sasha padded silently along the narrow, barely visible path that paralleled the rear stone wall. Dilly knew that path would take her to the wider logging trail that would eventually lead her back down the hill to Riverview Road.

The little mounds of still-damp pine needles under their feet released a comforting haylike scent and mingled with the earthy smell of mushrooms, bruised or broken by Dilly's sneakers or Sasha's pointed boots as she passed. From the tops of trees, crows cawed to each other, seeming either to take note of their progress or to recognize Sasha as some kind of kindred being, black-cloaked as she was.

I really feel at home in this forest, Dilly realized suddenly— *more than I do in Pasadena, even. Or in the desert. Or anyplace else on earth.*

It was the perfect place: just wild enough, just lonely enough to suit Dilly.

She wanted to ask Sasha if she felt the same about the forest, but she felt too shy.

"Have we finished *bonding* now?" Sasha asked plaintively, barely keeping the whine out of her voice. "Are you feeling a tad less loony? Can we go back to so-called civilization?" She brushed a pine needle from the sweep of her otherwise spotless coat.

"Sure," Dilly said, laughing. "Let's go home. And then I'll make you a nice hot cappuccino with our classic Italian coffee maker."

The Howells owned a vintage Mr. Coffee machine that rarely worked, so Sasha knew she was being teased. "Cruel child," she exclaimed haughtily. "Don't toy with me, Dillon. I'm warning you."

"As long as you don't forget who's boss around here," Dilly said, joking again. "I'm the queen of the snobs. Remember?"

"How can I forget?" Sasha asked, suddenly dead serious. "You're the one who dragged me up here, aren't you?"

Surprised, Dilly turned to face her friend. "But—but you like it up here in the forest. You know you do. Admit it," she said.

"I *mean* you dragged me up to Lake Luzerne," Sasha said with too much patience.

"I did not. Your wonderful Aunt Libby did that," Dilly said, heart pounding.

All of a sudden, they were having a fight. An actual fight!

"This wasn't Aunt Libby's bright idea," Sasha said flatly, sounding sure of herself. "If it was, she'd have told me by now why she wanted me here, wouldn't she? And she hasn't said a word. She just foisted me off on you, first chance she got. Mission accomplished."

"You weren't *foisted*," Dilly said, not quite sure what the word meant.

"I was absolutely foisted," Sasha snapped, flapping her cloak in irritation. "What's the matter, your majesty? Are you *lonesome* up here all by yourself?"

"Shut up," Dilly whispered. "You can just go home to Brooklyn right this second, as far as I'm concerned. And don't come back for my birthday, either. I don't want you here."

"Ooh, the queen has spoken," Sasha said, her voice matching Dilly's in its shakiness.

"Shut up!"

"I'm shutting," Sasha said. And she swept off down the hill toward Riverview Road.

"Well, hah," Dilly called after her. "Because that doesn't even make any sense, you big dope!"

Sasha yelled something back, but Dilly could not make out the words. "You dope, Sasha," she said again, whispering the words this time.

Hot tears blurred the trees around Dilly into a blinding shimmer of green.

Sasha called Dilly that night. "Can you talk?" she asked, her voice hushed.

A roaring sound—her quickened heartbeat—thrummed in Dilly's ears. "Yes," she whispered over the din, matching Sasha's serious, spylike tone.

Dilly wasn't expecting an apology, because Sasha wasn't the kind of person who said "I'm sorry" very often. Or ever, practically.

But Dilly knew that was because Sasha was a person who needed unpleasant things to be over with, once they had happened. Because, as Sasha had put it once, if you couldn't leave the bad things in life behind you, that meant they kind of kept on happening, didn't it? And then you could never stop worrying about anything.

"Where's your dad?" Sasha asked.

"Down in the basement, fiddling with the furnace. Why?"

"Because *I found something*," Sasha said, still keeping her voice low. It practically vibrated with excitement and importance, though.

"The letter?" Dilly asked, jumping to her feet.

"Not exactly," Sasha confessed. "But this is *big*. I searched Aunt Libby's desk while she was taking her walk just after dinner—and I found it in the bottom drawer! Something your mom wrote when she was a kid."

"Really?" Dilly asked. "What is it?"

"Kind of a diary, I guess," Sasha said, rustling some papers. "Only it's pretty short. Just a few pages."

A diary! "What does it say?" Dilly asked.

"Well, it's pretty weird—and I didn't really understand everything that's in it. But I'm not going to read it to you over the phone," Sasha said, indignant, as though there were anything better for a kid to do late on a Saturday night in Lake Luzerne.

"Come to my house, then," Dilly urged.

"It's eleven o'clock. Aunt Libby's already asleep," Sasha argued. "But even if it were still early, Dilly, she says she doesn't want me over there all the time."

"But you *have* to come," Dilly told her, frustrated. Because what was this, a law-abiding Sasha?

Yeah, right!

"I have to come?" Sasha replied coolly. "Gee, Dilly—you forgot to snap your fingers. I don't '*have to*' do anything."

"I'm sorry," Dilly said meekly—because even though Sasha never apologized, she expected other people to do it. At the drop of a hat, Dilly thought with some private bitterness.

"Okay, I forgive you," Sasha said. "But you can meet me

halfway, if you want to see the diary so much. Just tell your dad you're going for a walk."

"In the middle of the night?" Dilly asked, trying to keep her voice down.

"Well, it's just as late for me," Sasha pointed out. "Don't tell your dad anything. Sneak out, *Dully*—it'll be good for you. We can meet at that fence post that looks like it's about to fall down."

"Okay," Dilly said, darting a nervous glance toward her bedroom door, as if her father might be standing there listening to her every word.

But a clunk from the cellar and a muffled curse told her that he was still occupied.

"Five minutes," Dilly told Sasha.

Alone again in her bedroom and shivering with excitement eleven minutes later, Dilly began to read.

> *January 20, 1973*
> *Boston*
>
> *It has been exactly two months since I, Elspeth Halliburton Dillon, officially became an orphan. I feel less like one now, though, than I did when Sybil and Hallie were alive. Sybil and Hallie, Mother and Dad.*
>
> > *Rest in peace, and all that jazz.*
> > *Back up a minute—that sounded incredibly cold, and it's not the whole story about the way I feel. That is*

*just TOO COMPLICATED to go into! And I certainly
would never say such a thing out loud. It would hurt
Granny Tat too much.*

*But how come parents think that you're automati-
cally going to adore them when (A) They are too busy
telling each other how neither one has a drinking
problem to pay any attention to you, and (B) You
hardly ever see them, and (C) When you DO see
them, all they do is criticize you? "We don't do things
this way." "We don't do things like that."*

*Well, I don't get drunk and drive my car into a
tree without even considering what that might mean to
my one and only child!*

*Oh, sure, I loved them, but I have to say that I feel
happier (and more like a daughter) having Granny Tat
take care of me than I ever did when Sybil and Hallie
were alive. Even though I'm in boarding school.*

WHY?

*Probably because I know how much Granny Tat
loves me. And because I have Libby to keep me company. (Even if she has been kind of grouchy since we
got here. But most of the girls seem to really like her,
and Granny Tat says that pretty soon Libby will fit right
in.)*

*Thank God for Granny Tat, that's all I have to say.
And some day, Libby will say so too. Granny Tat is nifty.*

*Hallie used to say "nifty" a lot. Cocktail hour was
the niftiest. "Time to teach a lemon peel how to float,"*

he'd say, chuckling every time. Ha, ha, ha.

   Oops—gotta go. It's time for study hall.

   To be continued. . . .

June 23, 1973

Lake Luzerne

It is summer now, and we are back at the farm. Libby has been speaking to me again (sort of, anyway) since about last March. But we haven't really been hanging out much since we got here. I guess we just kind of need a break from each other. She's riding bikes with her little brother, and stuff. (I am so glad I don't have a brother.)

   Maybe going to school together wasn't such a good idea. Libby's doing really well there, though— better than I am in some classes, in fact.

   I asked LillyDill this morning why Granny Tat didn't just let me move in with her after Sybil and Hallie died. And how come I had to change schools at all, if I was still going to be in boarding school. LillyDill said that it would just have been TOO MUCH for Granny Tat to have a kid in the house all the time. After all, Granny Tat is an old lady in her 60s. It's not like she needs a thirteen-year-old kid racing up and down her fancy marble stairs and asking her how to spell "occurred," or how to figure out square roots, and stuff like that.

But she wants me to be nearby. She feels safer that way.

Also, LillyDill says that Granny Tat was messed up after the accident. Even though she and Hallie didn't really get along all that well, Granny Tat was a basket case when he died. She was NOT HERSELF, LillyDill says.

I will always be myself, NO MATTER WHAT.

(But I guess I was kind of messed up too.)

July 3, 1973
Lake Luzerne

Granny Tat and I are having this huge fight. She is NOT letting me hang out with the kids in town AT ALL this summer! NO FUN FOR ME!! And there are some really cute guys here, too!!! But NO-O-O-O, she is trying to keep me busy every single minute, day and night. She keeps coming up with these lame PROJECTS.

LillyDill says Granny Tat is just worried lately, worried that some other bad thing is going to happen to our family. But I say, "GET OVER IT!" (Not very loudly, though.)

At least Libby promised she will help me do the projects. She might as well, she says, because HER mom isn't letting her hang out with the local kids much, either. "Read," Mrs. Thorne tells Libby. "Improve your mind. Your life has changed, Elizabeth, so IMPROVE IT."

Libby says her life and her family has changed forever, thanks to me. (She doesn't actually say THANK
YOU, though.)

I am getting even with Granny Tat for being so
mean to me. I teased her by calling her "G.T." all day
yesterday, which is short for "gin and tonic," at least in
Boston. That's what Hallie liked to drink so she hates
that.

Also, I got out my guitar and sang folk songs while
Libby baked cookies.

"I never will marry, I'll be no man's wife!
I expect to live single,
ALL THE DAYS OF MY LIFE!!"

That song drives Granny Tat nuts, because she really wants me to marry and have lots of kids some day.
HAH!

Anyway, LillyDill is going to teach Libby and me
how to tie-dye T-shirts in the washing machine today!
She drove into Glens Falls this morning and bought
packages of white T-shirts at Sears, and dye, and
everything. She says our T-shirts will be psyche-DILL-
ic! GROAN.

But at least she is trying to make things more fun
for us.

We aren't telling Libby's mom about the tie-dying,
by the way, because Mrs. Thorne would just FREAK.

She always says, "We don't want any HIPPIES in Lake Luzerne, thank you very much!" which practically makes me and Libby pop, we are trying so hard not to laugh.

(I am glad to be laughing with Libby again.)

And anyway, Libby and I don't even call it Lake Luzerne anymore. We call it SNOB HILL! BECAUSE THAT'S WHAT IT IS!!

Here is something else I would never say out loud: Except for Libby, I hate being up here. It is BORING. I like it much better in Boston.

Well, except for Libby and the woods.

And the birch tree in the field.

And the front porch.

And, and, and . . .

Chapter Seventeen   The Thirty Years' War

Dilly and Sasha sat in silence on the Howells' sofa the next afternoon, staring into the empty fireplace as if invisible flames were hypnotizing them. The old farmhouse was quiet; Peter Howell had driven into Glens Falls for a long Sunday afternoon of tool browsing at Sears and grocery shopping at the Price Chopper.

The brass clock atop the old living room desk seemed to hiccup slightly, then it chimed three times.

It was as if she and Sasha were in a small, battered canoe this summer, floating on a turbulent river, Dilly thought, barely resisting the urge to start chewing her fingernails again, a habit she'd abandoned long ago. The canoe was their friendship: buoyant, but too easily tipped over. And the river was Sasha's newly volatile temper.

Sasha had always been a little touchy, true, but nothing like this.

Things seemed to be okay right this moment, Dilly said soothingly to herself. But how long was that going to last?

At Sasha's insistence, Dilly had finally "spilled every

bean," as her friend quaintly put it, and shared each of the Snob Hill papers she had unearthed during the past week. Perhaps this honesty would put them back on their old footing, Dilly fervently hoped.

But Sasha was taking her time coming up with a reaction. "So let me see if I've got this straight," she said, frowning.

That was always a bad beginning, Dilly thought, sinking lower into the lumpy sofa cushions.

"First," Sasha said, "you found a bunch of letters your mother and Aunt Libby sent each other when they were just about our age. And they basically say that your mom was getting lonely, and so Aunt Libby was going to have to go to school in Boston."

"Well, sort of," Dilly mumbled.

"Huh. And then you find the cookie recipe, and some competitive stuff about husbands that they wrote on a rainy day."

"Yeah, I guess."

"And then you find your old Christmas letters, which don't mean *anything*."

They mean something to me, Dilly thought fiercely. But she didn't say a word.

"And now," Sasha continued, her face darkening with anger, "we have this diary. And in it, your mother flat-out *announces* that maybe it wasn't such a great idea to make Aunt Libby change her life just so your spoiled brat of a mom could have some company."

"That's not exactly what—"

"So basically," Sasha interrupted, "Aunt Libby *was* kind of like your mom's pet. Just like she told your mother in those first letters. I always wondered why *she* got to go away to that fancy school in Boston while her brother—my extremely smart dad, in case you forgot!—was stuck here in Lake Luzerne. His parents just told Daddy to do the best he could, and that was that."

"He did great," Dilly said hurriedly. "Everyone's always saying so, Sasha."

Sasha's father did, indeed, appear to be making a great deal of money as a real estate broker. He was in partnership with his wife, Sasha's mom; they specialized in selling expensive city condos.

He hadn't visited his old home town in years.

"Don't sound so surprised," Sasha snapped. "He *happened* to do great in real estate. But maybe he would rather have done something else. Or maybe he could have done even better in real estate, if he'd had the same chances Aunt Libby did! He always thought so, anyway. It's always been this—this *thing* between them."

"So, what, are you mad at your aunt?" Dilly asked, confused.

"I'm mad at you! I'm mad at the world!"

"Well, that's just dumb," Dilly said heatedly. "Your grandmother and grandfather are the ones who made Libby go to Boston."

"And *your* grandmother is the one who came up with the brilliant idea in the first place. Because *that's the way the world is,* Dilly."

"Granny Tat was my *great*-grandmother," Dilly corrected her.

"Oh, who cares?" Sasha exploded, throwing a cushion across the room. "When she said 'Jump,' everyone said 'How high?' " That's the point. As if *'Little Orphan Elspeth'* were the only one worth worrying about."

"Granny Tat bossed my mom around, too," Dilly objected weakly.

"Just like you boss *me* around!" Sasha said, turning to face her friend. "Because that's the real reason why I'm up here, isn't it? I see it all now! And it's exactly like what happened to Aunt Libby."

"Huh?" Dilly's mind raced as she tried to cope with these words—which were both expected and unexpected—and to come up with a retort at the same time.

She was pretty sure she would never be able to.

"*One,* you get all bent out of shape because your mom wrote you a letter before she died," Sasha said, counting off the list of events on her fingers. "Then *two,* you pitch a hissy fit with poor Aunt Libby, who has probably been worrying about giving you that stupid letter for months, not that you care. *Three,* Aunt Libby gets all bent out of shape about your hissy fit, of course, and calls me to come and save the day. And *four,* I have to leave my *real* life and my *real* friends to come all the way up here to comfort you, queen of the snobs!"

Dilly stood up so quickly that her head seemed to keep on rising, as if it were a balloon filled with helium. "I thought *I* was your real friend," she said, barely managing to get the words out. "Or one of them, anyway."

Now Sasha was standing, too. A flicker of discomfort crossed her face, perhaps as she mentally replayed the words she'd just spoken, but she didn't back down. "You *were* one," she said in an unsteady voice. "Until I read those, that is," she added, pointing to the papers on the coffee table.

Dilly looked at the papers. All this grief, she thought—and she still hadn't found the letter from her mom.

Who knew what further misery *that* was going to cause?

"Those papers don't say anything about us, Sasha," she said shakily. "Not you and me. Everything in them happened years ago. And everything else, you just made up. It isn't the truth. Your thinking is all wrong."

Sasha shook her head as if she couldn't believe what she'd just heard. "And now, you're calling me a liar," she said, as if announcing it to the world.

"I'm not. You're my friend." The words came out in a whisper.

Sasha's pale face turned even whiter, making her look as if she were about to faint, but her short black hair stood up like a collection of exclamation points. "*Shut up.* Stop trying to make me feel bad," she said, her voice harsh with anger. "It's not going to work."

"I'm not trying to make you feel bad," Dilly protested. "And I didn't mean to make you come to Lake Luzerne, either. Not on purpose, anyway. It just happened."

"Everything always just happens, is that it?" Sasha asked sarcastically. "Everyone with 'Dillon' in their name *just happens* to get their own way? In Lake Luzerne, at least? No wonder my father hates it up here!"

"Well, if he hates it here so much, how come he sends you up to visit Libby all the time?" Dilly asked, throwing her hands in the air in frustration. "I thought you said there was this *thing* between them."

"Well, yeah, but he loves her! And he loves Lake Luzerne, too. That's why he finally let me come up for visits."

"Your dad loves Lake Luzerne," Dilly repeated, as if daring Sasha to hear her own words.

"Why shouldn't he?" Sasha cried. "Our family has been living here for almost two hundred and fifty years!"

"But he also hates it," Dilly said, echoing Sasha's earlier statement.

"I guess," Sasha said, her anger fading a little. "I think it reminds him of fights with his dad, or something. Sometimes, I think that Aunt Libby is only able to appreciate the place because she got to go away when she was so young."

"Well, I just found out that my mom loved and hated being

here, too," Dilly said, nodding her head in the direction of the Snob Hill papers. "So I guess my mother and your father have something in common."

Sasha made a snorting sound, but at least she was listening.

"And Libby hated my mom for a while, when they were our age," Dilly continued, her heart thudding. "But they ended up staying friends—because Libby loved her, too. Just like my mother loved Granny Tat, even though she drove her crazy at times. I even think my mom loved Hallie and Sybil, in spite of what she said in her diary. So maybe it's not the end of the world if you think you hate me, Sasha. You'll never have something perfect to love—or some*body*—except in your imagination."

Dilly crossed her fingers behind her back, wondering what Sasha's response would be. Probably that Dilly was sounding like a self-help book from the library, one that was way overdue.

Sasha gave a tiny shrug and picked at the nail polish on one of her thumbs. "I don't *hate* you," she finally conceded. "But—but doesn't it seem like everyone who has ever come up here has spent a whole lot of time walking around mad? Your mother, Aunt Libby, me, you. It's like there's this curse on the place."

Dilly gave a matching shrug and even managed a tiny smile. "There's no curse," she said. "It's just been the thirty years' war, I guess—even though nobody really knew it was going on," she said. *"The Dillons against the Thornes."*

"*The Thornes against the Dillons,*" Sasha corrected her. "We were here first."

Dilly gave a shaky laugh. "Have it your way, Sasha."

"I intend to. Starting right this very minute, in fact."

Dilly held her breath. Starting right this very minute? Did that mean Sasha was about to walk out the door—and out of her life forever?

Stay, stay! she wanted to beg. *I'm sorry my mother bossed your aunt around. I'm sorry Granny Tat bossed* everyone *around. I'm sorry if I ever bossed* you *around. But the war is over, see? And it's been over for a long, long time.*

But she didn't say any of these things.

Sasha sighed, chewed on her lower lip as if she were trying to decide something, and glanced over at the clock on the desk.

Three-forty.

Dilly waited in silence; it was the most difficult thing she'd ever done.

Sasha slid her a look, and then smiled a silent apology. "I guess you're not the only one who can throw a hissy fit, are you, *Dillon?*" she told Dilly.

Dilly grinned. "I guess not," she agreed, uncrossing her fingers and wiggling them slightly to get the feeling back.

Sasha shrugged again, but comically this time. Then she

leaned over and rummaged through the papers on the coffee table.

"What are you looking for?" Dilly asked, trying to sound casual.

"That crazy cookie recipe," Sasha said. "Because I am starving, Dilly my friend. And if you've got the ingredients, I've got the time."

"Well, I have nothing *but* time," Dilly said, laughing. "And I hope I have the ingredients. I'm not sure about those dry-roasted peanuts, though."

Sasha smiled. "We can always make up our own recipe, can't we?"

"Absolutely," Dilly agreed. "We can call them *Cookies for Kids Who Decide Things for Themselves.*"

"Let's go, then."

"You got it!"

Chapter Eighteen

To Make a Short Story Long

Dilly woke up early the next day. Her small, pink-papered bedroom was already warm, and it wasn't even seven A.M. The house was very still.

The silence was a relief after the fight she'd had yesterday with Sasha, although of course it wasn't perfectly quiet outside. Crows called jeeringly to each other across fields and forests, and an empty logging truck rattled by on Riverview Road, going at top speed.

Dilly swung out of bed and padded downstairs for an early breakfast, not bothering to put on either her robe or slippers. She could hear water running in the downstairs bathroom her dad always used.

Dilly walked straight through the kitchen, out the kitchen door, and onto the porch, even though she was wearing torn old sweatpants and a shrunken T-shirt that had seen better days, as Mrs. Oller would have put it. The porch's gray-painted floorboards were warm under Dilly's bare feet.

She stretched, then walked to the edge of the porch and sat down. The lawn was still dewy, she saw, but just barely—

another sign that today would be a scorcher. Maybe she and Sasha would go splash around in the river! They could try to find a deep spot and bob around in that big black inner tube her dad had unearthed in the garage.

If Sasha hasn't decided to leave town, that is, Dilly warned herself.

Looking south across Riverview Road and the big field, and beyond the trees that surrounded that field, she could track the winding path of the Hudson River by its mist as a white cloudlike vapor rose from the slow-moving water.

Dilly looked down admiringly at her feet. Sasha had painted her toenails midnight blue after they'd finished baking cookies yesterday evening, and Dilly had slept with her feet poking out from under the covers so as not to risk smudging the polish. Now, her feet were resting on the massive granite block that served as a step up to the porch.

This reminded Dilly of an old photograph that Libby had shown her the summer before: Standing in front of the stone retaining wall that enclosed the farmhouse's front lawn, raising it up from street level, several nineteenth-century Thornes stood dour and stolid, posing for a family portrait. Oddly Sasha-like, they were unsmiling, although obviously aware that they were being photographed. The men wore floppy black ties, hats, vests, and jackets, and the women's white aprons were immaculate, Dilly recalled.

The photograph was probably taken just before the property changed hands in 1889, Libby had told her.

For some reason, Dilly remembered the moment Libby had said this very clearly.

But most of all she remembered the photographed stone wall itself.

The wall was a lot cleaner looking in the old days. No weeds sprouted between the immense stone slabs and the lawn as they did now. In some fundamental way, however, that wall was exactly the same now as it had been well over one hundred years ago—or two hundred years ago, for that matter, before photography was even invented.

A chill zipped up Dilly's back as she thought about this: The wall was never going to change, not until some developer's bulldozer destroyed it forever.

If she let that happen.

Things changed; all of the people in the photograph had died. Granny Tat was gone. Even beautiful Elspeth Dillon Howell was dead. But the stone wall—built over who knew how many years, and at what human cost—endured, impassive.

Dilly could stand precisely where the people in that old photograph had stood. In fact, she *had* stood there, in their imaginary footprints, wondering if anything felt different—if *she* felt different, standing there.

But she hadn't felt any kind of a vibe at all, no matter how hard she tried.

That didn't seem right.

I hope Sasha stays—at least for a while, she thought. *I hope Sasha* _wants_ *to stay.*

"Oh, there you are," Dilly's father said, poking his head out the kitchen door. "Want me to make you some eggs?"

"Yes, I do," Dilly said emphatically, getting to her feet.

"Nice outfit," her dad observed with a grin.

"Glad you like it," Dilly replied, and she whirled around and around, pausing only to strike a pose in the clear Adirondack morning.

Mrs. Oller came to clean every Monday afternoon when they were at the farm, though she had skipped coming the previous week, since the Howells had just arrived. Dilly and her father had learned to make themselves scarce while the Lake Luzerne–born woman whizzed through the house, vacuum cleaner and yellow plastic wash bucket in hand. Dilly and her dad usually drove to nearby Corinth for lunch and some shopping.

There was always time for Dilly to have a visit with Mrs. Oller before leaving the house, however. Marti Oller loved hearing about California and Dilly's friends there; she always remembered their names from one year to the next, which pleased Dilly. Mrs. Oller also liked discussing whether or not anything unusual had happened in either Pasadena or Lake Luzerne that the other should know about.

"Were there any earthquakes this year?" Mrs. Oller asked Dilly hopefully, after their usual warm greeting. Her long fuzzy duster flashed along the dark beams in the low kitchen ceiling.

"Just a little jolt. A vase fell off the mantelpiece and broke," Dilly said, seated at the table. She had just finished stripping the beds and gathering damp towels and bath mats from the bathrooms, and her dad was in his study, making a few phone calls before they left for Corinth.

"How awful," Mrs. Oller said, her blue eyes sparkling. "We had a really nasty winter up here—a roof on one of the camps down along River Road caved in from all the snow."

"That's terrible," Dilly said, and they exchanged sunny smiles.

"Don't worry, the place was empty at the time," Mrs. Oller said reassuringly, jabbing the duster into a corner so hard that Dilly almost felt sorry for any spider who might be lurking there.

Dilly hadn't been too concerned about the collapsed roof, since she didn't know the people involved, but Mrs. Oller's motherly tone was part of their relationship. After all, Marti Oller volunteered for Libby Thorne at the library when she could manage to, and Libby had been Elspeth Howell's best friend.

That was the way things worked in Lake Luzerne.

"Which *reminds* me," Mrs. Oller said, striking her brow dramatically at her own forgetfulness. "I came in to air things out before you and your father arrived. You know, to make up the beds, and dust, and so on. Hy opens the house each spring, of course, but that doesn't mean he's about to lift a finger to tidy things up—not that he should, him being a plumber and all. You wouldn't want to go paying someone a plumber's rates just to change a few beds."

"No way," Dilly agreed.

"So anyway," Mrs. Oller continued in her leisurely way, "I was here a couple of weeks ago, and it was coming down buckets. No surprise there. But to make a short story long, I'd washed the curtains in your bedroom, Dilly, and I was hanging them up again when I noticed something a little out of the ordinary."

"What was that?" Dilly asked idly, only half paying attention.

"There was a letter sitting on your bureau, propped up against the mirror. The envelope said *'Dilly'* on it, plain as day, but there wasn't a stamp on it or anything. Just a big glob of sealing wax on the back. The letter looked important, maybe even valuable."

Dilly goggled at her, but Mrs. Oller didn't notice, busy as she was with her duster.

"So I guess that means somebody came into the house and left it for you," she continued, "which is kind of a funny thought. Maybe it was Libby who left it—I haven't had the chance to ask her about it yet. Only, now that I think about it, the handwriting wasn't hers. Anyway, I decided that I'd better just take the darn thing home. You know, hang on to it for you, Dilly—until you folks arrived. I didn't want some strange repair person who might get called to come in and fix something to go waltzing off with it."

Feeling as if she were frozen to her seat, Dilly tried to clear her throat. "Where—where is it?" she asked hoarsely. "Where is the letter now?"

"Right here," Mrs. Oller said, pausing in her work to pull a thick, cream-colored envelope out of her capacious handbag with a flourish. "I sure hope it wasn't something that needed taking care of right away. I meant to bring it by last week, but you know how *that* goes."

Dilly saw a flash of bold familiar handwriting and felt the lump of sealing wax at the same moment she heard a floorboard creak; her dad was walking through the living room. He would be in the kitchen any second.

Dilly did *not* want him to see her mother's letter—until she was sure that it was something she wanted to share.

"Thanks," she told Mrs. Oller hastily, taking the envelope. Her fingers grazed the slick red sealing wax lump on its back as she slipped her mother's letter into the kitchen table's silverware drawer. "I'll put it in here for later," she said softly.

Marti Oller looked at the drawer, then looked at Dilly— and winked! She obviously understood that this letter was to be kept a secret from Peter Howell.

Dilly found herself winking back just as her father entered the room. Mrs. Oller probably figured that the letter was from some mysterious local boyfriend who had conned the plumber into delivering it, she thought.

Dilly almost laughed out loud.

Chapter Nineteen  Only a Letter

Dilly knew that if she had been able to open her mother's letter right away, she probably would have. Instead, trapped in the Lumina with her father for three whole hours, she stared moodily out of the open car window as Peter Howell steered down Lake Luzerne's main street, heading south toward Corinth. He adjusted and then readjusted the air-conditioning controls, though nothing more than a warm steady breeze was coming from the car's vents.

"It still doesn't work. It hasn't worked for the past two years," Dilly said, watching the library roll by.

Libby. She had accused Libby of hiding the letter.

Sasha. She was dying to tell Sasha what actually had happened to it.

"But the AC *should* work. I got it fixed again," her dad fretted, punching the dashboard button once more. Harder, this time, as if that might convince it to turn on.

This was one of the big differences between men and women, Dilly thought moodily. Men had these firm ideas about the way things should be, and if they weren't that way, then look out—they'd *make* them that way.

Sometimes this attitude worked, but other times it was just plain dumb, at least in Dilly's opinion. Like with that stupid air conditioner, she brooded. Or with the way her dad decided they should stick to their old routine whether they really wanted to or not.

If a man got a letter, he would open it. Case closed.

Because that's what you did with letters!

Women, on the other hand—or even girls—were more flexible about things, it seemed to Dilly.

They were realists.

Take the example of the letter from her mother, Dilly thought, trying to consider the subject objectively.

But this couldn't be done, not even for a moment. Instead, and in a very nonobjective way, Dilly suddenly pictured the sealed letter as waiting for her in the gloom of the silverware drawer, its beady little imaginary eyes shining with malice. Perhaps when she finally opened that drawer, the letter would leap out at her like one of those springy joke "snakes" that people hid inside a fake box of chocolates.

The letter from her mom *would* have to pop up just when she'd begun to feel a little bit happier about being here, and when things were finally—if temporarily—going okay with Sasha.

What a joke.

That letter would prove to be a flat-out disaster: the beginning of the end, as far as her own peace of mind was concerned.

No, wait—get serious, Dilly told herself sternly. Now, *she* was thinking wrong!

It was only a letter, and she had lots of choices of what to do with it. She could ignore it, for instance. Or she could destroy it—tear it up, as Libby had once guessed that she might do, or burn it, or flush it down the toilet, or bury it in the woods.

"River's pretty today," her father remarked as they cruised alongside the Hudson, heading toward Corinth. The Sacandaga River merged with the Hudson just south of Lake Luzerne, and the Hudson was wider now. A heat haze seemed to be rising from it, and Dilly could see tiny people across the river bustling around on their toy docks, getting ready to take their motorboats out.

Snob Hill had always scoffed at motorboats; sailboats were considered much "niftier," although sailing was impossible along this part of the Hudson.

But Dilly was still like Ratty, in a way, and any boat at all sounded like fun to her. Maybe she'd even buy a motorboat some day! Why not, if she could afford it? "It sure *is* pretty," she agreed, since her dad seemed to be waiting for a reply.

This contribution to the conversation satisfied him.

Dilly's thoughts returned to the letter. One of her choices was to read it—read it, and then keep and treasure it, Dilly lectured herself, trying to be adult and reasonable. After all, hadn't Libby practically promised that it would be stuffed full of love and inspiration? Perhaps that one piece of paper would make it up to her somehow for not having had a mother for the last six years.

Yeah, right.

But even if the letter couldn't do that, it might answer some of the questions she would have during the *next* six years, Dilly told herself. Questions about what kind of present to give her teachers at the end of the school year; about how to make scrambled eggs the correct way; about how best to take care of Snob Hill.

Questions about how to survive having had a fight with your best friend. Her mom must have been an expert on that.

The letter wouldn't answer every question; Dilly knew that much from having read the *other* Snob Hill papers. Learning more about your family was like working on a big jigsaw puzzle that you could never hope to complete, she thought suddenly.

You could finish enough to see the basic picture, though. Patterns, and so on.

Maybe she should *not* open that letter, though, Dilly argued silently. There was no way that it could be as good as she hoped it might be—as it needed to be.

Maybe her mother's letter would be filled with makeup advice, Dilly thought, cringing in advance: *"Darling Dilly, I'd advise you to aim either for smoky dark eyes and light lipstick or for a vivid mouth and softer, subtler eyes."* Were fashion magazine article headlines going to have to be her words to live by?

Or maybe her mom would complain about Dilly's dad in the letter. After all, her father had said that Elle could be a handful, hadn't he? *"Peter is driving me absolutely crazy,"* Dilly imagined her mother's letter telling her. *"Never trust a man, sweetie. Like the old folk song says, I should have lived single— all the days of my life!"*

And what was she, Dilly, supposed to do with crazy advice such as that?

"We're here," Dilly's father said, gliding into a parking spot directly across from Jack's, the Corinth restaurant at which they always ate.

It was after four-thirty when they finally returned home; Peter Howell had decided that he needed to stop by the Glens Falls Sears yet again, to exchange a tool he'd bought the day before.

Marti Oller's truck was gone when they pulled into the driveway, the front porch was swept, and the farmhouse kitchen gleamed its welcome as Dilly and her dad carried the grocery sacks straight through to the pantry. Dilly hardly dared even to glance at the kitchen table for fear that she might give its secret away.

"Open me, open me!" the letter seemed to be howling.

It was cool inside the old house, downstairs, at least, and

that was a relief. Dilly and her father put the groceries away in silence, although Dilly's heart thudded with anxiety. Peter Howell was tired from both the heat and the afternoon's dull chores, and Dilly didn't think she could have spoken a word if someone offered her a hundred brand-new dollar bills.

"I'm going to go stretch out on the sofa and read," Dilly's father told her after washing his hands at the kitchen sink and pouring them both icy glasses of water to drink.

"Okay," Dilly whispered. She cleared her throat, took a sip of water, and tried again. "Okay," she repeated. "I'm going to go down the road to visit Libby and Sasha for a while."

She had not known that was her plan until she uttered the words.

Once she'd said them aloud, however, it was obvious to her that seeing Libby and Sasha was precisely what she had to do.

And she would bring the unopened letter with her.

After all, Libby Thorne had been her mother's best friend—and Sasha was *her* best friend.

They were the only two people in the world who could tell her what to do, now that the letter had been found.

Chapter Twenty  What If

The car was in Libby's driveway, thank goodness.

Looking a lot more confident than she was feeling, Dilly strode across Libby's summer-parched lawn. Would Sasha still be there, or would she have taken off for the city? And would Libby be forgiving enough even to talk about the letter?

Libby's front door opened before Dilly's foot even hit the first porch step. Dilly hesitated on the gravel path.

"So you found it," Libby said calmly, wiping her hands on a yellow dish towel as she stood in the doorway. It looked as though she were just cleaning up from working in the garden. Her pumpkin-colored T-shirt and khaki shorts were soiled, and her knees were dirty. She was barefoot, having apparently removed her shoes and socks after gardening, and her feet looked pale.

Dilly glanced down at the envelope she was holding. "I *kind of* found it," she said.

"Where was it? Had it fallen behind your bureau?" Libby asked, tilting her head in polite inquiry.

Dilly forced herself to raise her eyes. "No," she said. "Mrs.

Oller saw it on my bureau when she was cleaning just before we came. She thought it looked valuable, so she took it home with her for safekeeping. She didn't get around to giving it to me until today."

"Ah," Libby said, nodding as if a puzzle had been solved. "I put Elspeth's letter in your bedroom a couple of weeks ago, but then on the day you arrived, I got nervous about you just *finding* it there. So I thought maybe I should leave a note on the kitchen door preparing you for it. I guess I should have checked to make sure that it was still where I left it, but it never occurred to me that it might not be."

"Anyway, it wasn't there," Dilly said, stating the obvious.

Libby sighed and slapped a fly away with the yellow towel. "Well, I guess you'd better come in," she finally said.

Dilly followed Libby into the living room, still clutching the unopened letter—which was creased from her grip now, and damp where her fingers had been touching it. "Did Sasha leave?" she asked.

"No, she's still here," Libby said. "She's been taking the world's longest shower, but I'm sure she'll be down here the second she hears your voice." Libby gestured toward the sofa, and Dilly sat down gingerly. She put the letter in the exact center of Libby's coffee table, relieved to let it go.

Maybe she could just leave it there forever, she found herself thinking. She could offer to go outside and pull a few weeds or pick some radishes, and then everything would be okay with Libby again, and they could forget that the whole thing had ever happened.

"What would you like to drink?" Libby asked.

"Water, thanks," Dilly told her. She didn't really think she could swallow a drop of anything at all, but Lake Luzerne hospitality demanded that she allow Libby to bring her something.

Ice trays rattled in the kitchen for a few seconds, and Dilly heard the sound of running water coming both from the kitchen and from upstairs in the bathroom, which meant that Sasha was still enjoying her shower.

Libby reappeared in the living room with two glasses on an old tole tray. "Well," she said, after she had sat down. She looked quizzically at the letter on the coffee table.

If that letter were a rattlesnake, Dilly thought, its tail would be up and buzzing right now. "Well," she echoed weakly. She cleared her throat and then forced herself to take a sip of the water.

She wanted to talk about the letter, sure, but first, she needed to apologize for what she had said the week before. And it would be better—and easier—to do that *before* Sasha made her grand entrance.

But apologizing to Libby was turning out to be even harder than Dilly had imagined it would be. Suddenly, however, Dilly remembered the words that young Elspeth Dillon had written so boldly in her diary: *"I hope that I always have the guts to do the right thing, no matter what."*

Her mother had never said, *"I'll do the right thing—if it's easy!"*

Well, *she* could do the right thing, Dilly told herself. "Before we talk about my mom's letter," she said, her mouth suddenly dry, despite her sip of water, "there's something that I have to say to you. I want to apologize, Libby—but I don't know how, exactly."

"What are you apologizing for?" Libby asked, as if trying to help.

"I—I was wrong to say that you were interested in my dad. You know, romantically," Dilly added, miserable. She stared down at the floor, heat rising in her cheeks as her vision blurred.

"But what if I *were* interested?" Libby asked, sounding as if this was a casual question.

Dilly's world stopped for a moment. She had not expected this reply.

"Would that be pathetic, Dilly?" Libby asked, still cool. "Because I'd like to know, if that's what you really think."

Dilly cleared her throat again. What *did* she really think? "No, it wouldn't be pathetic. Of course not," she finally said. "But I guess I'd be kind of like—in shock, I guess, if you and my dad got together. Not because it was you, though. I'd be in shock if he started dating *anyone* seriously, to be perfectly honest."

Libby laughed. "That's fair enough," she said.

"It's nothing personal," Dilly assured her weakly.

Libby nodded her head. "Duly noted."

Her heart pounding in her ears, Dilly quickly reviewed this unexpected conversation. "But—but *are* you interested in dating my father?" she asked.

"It would certainly be news to him if I were," Libby said, not really answering Dilly's question. "It's even a fairly recent idea for me. You're the one who got me thinking about it, in fact. Still feel like apologizing to me, Dilly?" Libby asked, a wry smile on her lips.

Dilly gave this some thought. "I guess so," she said at last. "I had no right to say what I did. So yes, I apologize."

And now—shut up, she told herself. *Say you're sorry, period. No excuses.*

"Well, thank you for your apology," Libby said, sounding formal. She sipped from her own glass of water.

Dilly waited for more, but nothing came. "Are you going to do anything about it? Let him know how you feel?" she finally asked, not able to stand the silence any longer.

Libby shrugged a freckled shoulder. "I don't know how I feel," she said. "Anyway, I have my loyalty to *her* to think about," she added, nodding her head in the direction of Elspeth Howell's letter.

The letter.

"Even after the way she *treated* you?" Dilly asked.

"The way she treated me?"

Dilly blushed. After all, she thought wildly, Libby didn't know anything at all about her having discovered the various

Snob Hill papers. "I—I mean I'm sure you and my mom had lots of ups and downs through the years. So it's nice that you're still so loyal to her."

"They were nothing, our fights. Not in the long run, Dilly."

"So you forgive her?"

"There's nothing to forgive!" Libby exclaimed. "Except maybe me not being with her when she died. I hope Elle forgave me that."

"My mom has been gone for six whole years. And he's lonely, my dad is," Dilly said, hating to utter the words—but feeling that she must.

"Well, loneliness is the human condition," Libby said softly, shrugging. "So, what about that letter? Why haven't you opened it?"

Dilly shook her head, mute.

"Why?" Libby repeated.

"I'm afraid," Dilly confessed, blurting out something she hadn't even known. "I mean, what if it's not good enough? Or what if *I'm* not good enough? The letter might tell me that she wants me to be a ballet dancer, or some other impossible thing. She loved ballet, didn't she?"

Libby laughed.

"Or—or what if it says something really dumb?" Dilly continued, emboldened. "Then that's what I'll always have to remember about her."

"Who said something really dumb?" Sasha asked from the foot of the stairs, rubbing her damp hair with a small red towel until it stood up in tufts. She wore a long NYU T-shirt that clung a little to her still-damp thighs. "Don't tell me I missed something good!"

"You didn't miss a thing," Libby told her niece as she flopped down into an easy chair. "Dilly just found a letter her mother wrote her before she died, and she's afraid to open it. That's all."

That's all? Dilly couldn't believe anyone could put something so—so *intense* in such a casual way.

"Then I'll open it," Sasha said, reaching for the letter.

Libby swatted her niece's hand away. "It'll be Dilly or no one," she announced. She and Sasha turned and looked at Dilly expectantly.

"I just don't know," Dilly whispered.

Libby tilted her head, preparing to ask Dilly a question. "If you took a chance and opened that letter, would you feel any worse than the way you do right now?" she asked.

"I might."

"But you might not," Sasha said, looking as if she would like to grab the letter and run back upstairs with it, locking every door behind her so that she could read it undisturbed.

Libby laughed again and shook her head. "Poor Dilly. I keep forgetting that you never really knew Elspeth, in a funny sort of way. I don't think she'd be capable of disappointing you, honey. She loved you very, very much."

"Yeah, right," Dilly said, jumping to her feet. "She loved

me, and so she died! How was I supposed to grow up without a mother, did she ever bother to think about that?"

Even Sasha looked startled at this outburst, and Libby blinked her surprise. "You sound like you're about five years old, Dilly," she remarked after a moment.

"I'm six, to be exact," Dilly snapped—and then she laughed a little, feeling sheepish. "I mean, I *was* six. When Mummie died."

"But you don't still blame her for dying, do you?" Libby asked, her voice soft.

"I'd say part of her does," Sasha said. She gazed at Dilly as if her friend were Exhibit A in an unusually interesting science project.

"Part of me still does," Dilly admitted. "It's gotten to be kind of a habit, I guess."

"Well, get over it," Sasha said crisply. "It's not like it's the truth, or anything."

"And Elle *did* bother to think about dying," Libby said, arguing in her old friend's behalf. "She thought about it for a couple of years, as a matter of fact."

"Well, what good did all that thinking do *me*?" Dilly asked, not quite wanting to be robbed of her anger—and not waiting for an answer this time. "Did it help me when I heard my dad cry at night after she died and I didn't know what to do?"

Libby and Sasha stared at her. Libby looked as if she were about to cry herself, hearing this.

"Did it help him make me a good Halloween costume each year?" Dilly continued, almost buzzing with remembered rage. "No! I had to wear those horrible store-bought costumes when I was little, while all my friends had moms who made costumes for them. *They* got to be Hershey bars or rock stars, but I always had to be the same old princess wearing a scuzzy pink dress that didn't even fit! I swear that my dad bought five of those costumes at the same time, only in different sizes. Mummie should have planned things out better. She *knew* my dad couldn't sew."

Libby shook her head, amazed. "But—but Elspeth couldn't sew either, Dilly."

"She could have learned," Dilly shot back. "That's what mothers are supposed to do, *Libby*. And who was supposed to braid my hair, if I happened to feel like growing it out? Look at me," she demanded of Libby and Sasha, pulling her short locks straight for a moment. *"Does this look like a French braid to you?"*

"No," Libby said meekly.

"Nuh-uh," Sasha chimed in. *"Thank goodness,"* she added under her breath.

"Well, not to me either!" Dilly shouted. Something tickled her face, and she reached up to find that tears were streaming down her cheeks. "Oh, great! And now you guys are probably going to tell me to shut up and stop feeling sorry for myself, aren't you?" Dilly asked Libby and Sasha, choking back a sob.

"No. I think you should keep on talking," Libby said. She

looked, even more, as though she were about to start crying, too.

"I wouldn't mind it if you stopped *yelling*," Sasha commented shakily.

"Well, I don't have anything more to yell about, so fine!" Dilly announced—seconds before she broke down completely. "I'm just terrible," she sobbed, her face buried in her hands. "I don't know why I said all that stuff. I mean, I miss Mummie and everything, but not for the reasons I said. I'm so sorry."

"That's okay," Sasha said, on her knees at Dilly's feet, now, tears of sympathy filling her lower lashes. "I'm sorry, too. And I don't even know why!"

"Oh, Dilly," Libby said, weeping openly as she leaned over to take the girl into her arms and hug her tight. "We're all sorry, darling. We're just so very, very sorry."

Twenty minutes later, the three of them had recovered enough to face the letter once more. "Do you want me to tear it up?" Sasha asked, glaring at the letter through red-rimmed eyes.

Dilly shook her head, exhausted.

"Well, what, then?"

"I want Libby to open it up and read it," Dilly said, making her decision as she spoke. "Sasha, you and I will go upstairs and wash our faces, and when we come back down, Libby can tell us what it says. If you think I should know, Libby."

"Okay. Go."

Chapter Twenty-One  **Dear Dilly**

May 28, 1996

Dear Dilly,

    I don't know exactly how old you'll be when you're reading this, but I want you to know that this is the only so-called "future mail" I have written you. No more surprises after this, at least from me. I say that because I have mixed feelings about writing you this letter at all. I'm not sure how I would have felt if Sybil (my mother) had written such a letter to me. I would probably have been furious. Maybe I'd even have ripped it to shreds! But she died so suddenly that she never got the chance.

    Anyway, a few people seem to think this letter is a good idea, so here goes.

    To begin with, I want to tell you a couple of things about my illness and get that out of the way. I was always a little bit afraid of dying young, since my own parents did. And it turns out that I <u>am</u> dying young. But my parents' car accident could have been avoided if

Hallie hadn't been drinking. (I hope that news doesn't shock you!) That is not to say that I blame them anymore for dying. It's just that they could have taken better care of themselves.

My own illness is not the kind that could have been discovered any sooner than it was, and it turned out to be difficult, and then impossible, to treat. But we all did everything we could, that's my point. I could not have taken better care of myself—or been better cared for.

Your father has been a hero to me.

The most important thing, though, is that I want to tell you not to be afraid—of illness, even of dying young, just because I did. I have a feeling that you will be more like Granny Tat, who made it to an amazing eighty-nine years of age. (I know you'll be happier and more at ease in this world than she ever was, though. I can already tell that you have a foundation of happiness in you, Dilly!)

Having said that, though, I will also remind you to take extra-good care of yourself, because Daddy and I love you as much as I hope you will come to love yourself. And if something ever does go wrong, you be the squeakiest wheel on the block until you get the care you deserve. Forget manners, forget modesty, and be a pain in the blankety-blank neck, if you have to! It's your life, and good health is worth fighting for.

May 30, 1996

That's enough about that.

You are six years old as I write these words, Dilly, and I think that you are scared, and confused, and sad, and even angry with me, even though you don't know why. But I hope you never regret having had those feelings or feel guilty about them. You <u>should</u> be angry! I'm sad and angry, too, not only because I'm sick, but because your daddy and I are being cheated out of our lives together, and most of all because you and I are being robbed of <u>our</u> lives together.

I will not be there for so many things—for the traditional fun things, such as birthday parties, and trick-or-treating, and school plays, and Christmas mornings. I'll also miss the goofy pleasures, though, such as pulling you out of class early so we can sneak off together for a matinée and a hot fudge sundae, or treating you to the prettiest, laciest nightgown in the world, <u>just</u> <u>because</u>, or braiding your beautiful hair.

I'll miss being at the farm with you and Daddy each summer, watching you as you discover the blueberry bush, the birch tree, the forest trails.

June 2, 1996

But I'll even miss the bad things we would have shared, Dilly, such as the times I'd have held your forehead when you had the stomach flu, or the times you

would have hated me for making you work harder on
your homework, or the times I would have told you,
"No, you cannot wear those shoes with that dress,
young lady," and, "No, you may <u>not</u> stay out as late as
all your friends do."

Not that I believe that lame old everyone-is-
staying-out-late story for a single minute! Even Granny
Tat never fell for that one.

I'll miss the sound of your bedroom door slamming in my face as you vow never, ever to speak to me
again.

And I'll miss things I can't even imagine now. Will
you grow up to be a quilter, an adorer of Abyssinian
kittens, a climber of mountains, or a player of champi-
onship tennis? Will you volunteer at an orphanage in
Mexico, or discover a new medicine that will save
people pain, or—rob a bank?

Don't rob a bank. That's a no-no, Dilly-dilly!

June 4, 1996

Apart from <u>that</u> brilliant advice, there are only a
few things I have to say:

Love other people, and listen to them. Don't be
afraid of silence. Cherish your friends as if they were
the most precious things in the world, because they
are your treasure. Find work that you can give your
heart to, and then do it well. Be a creator, not a

destroyer. Try to erase the difference between the way you see yourself and the way the world sees you. Forgive other people when they hurt you, but don't let them hurt you again.

Help care for the world and the people in it. They are counting on you.

Don't talk about your good deeds, though.

Know that you are deeply loved.

Love others just as deeply.

Keep moving that body.

Think about things.

Read.

June 12, 1996

I'm going to stop working on this letter, Dilly, because I've said most of what I wanted to say. Also, I am getting tired, and I want to make sure this gets officially sealed by my day nurse and sent off properly to my dear friend Libby, who will eventually be the one to give it to you. Libby has always been my rock. If you're lucky, you'll have a friend like that someday.

I hope you have as wonderful a life as I did, dear Dilly.

Look around you. Isn't it a beautiful world?

Love,

Mummie

Dilly, Sasha, and Libby were all crying again by the time Libby finished reading the letter aloud. "Oh, Dilly—I still miss her," Libby admitted, wiping away some tears with the back of her hand.

"Me too," Dilly said, hiccuping.

"Me too," Sasha said. "And I didn't even know her."

"Hang on, I'm going to go get some tissues," Libby told the girls, getting up from the sofa. "You should see your faces! I just wish I had a camera."

"Yeah," Sasha said, trying to wipe her eyes on her short T-shirt sleeves. "Because this is definitely a moment to remember, Aunt Libby."

"And you should see *your* face," Dilly called after Libby, because the light swipes of mascara Libby used each morning had somehow turned into menacing smudges under her eyes. "You look like a football player—only smaller."

"And a whole lot meaner, of course," Sasha added, sniffling. "You should have seen how she made me work in the garden all afternoon. And there were *bugs* out there."

Libby came back into the living room giggling and crying at the same time. She handed a box of tissues to the girls, and Dilly took a couple. She blew her nose with a loud honk. "Oof," she said, sagging back against the navy blue cushions. "I feel like I just fell down a mountain."

"Me too," Libby said, collapsing into her chair once more.

"Knock, knock," Peter Howell's voice called out from

behind Libby's screen door. "Libby? Dilly?"

Dilly, Sasha, and Libby exchanged guilty looks, as if they were kids who'd been caught in their secret hideout. "Just a second," Dilly called out, and she scooped up all the pages of her mother's letter and slid them under a sofa cushion.

"I'll let him in," Libby said, wiping frantically at her mascara smudges. She shot Dilly a panicky look.

"Better just do it," Sasha advised. "We can say you got a black eye fighting with some lady who was arguing about an overdue book."

Libby giggled. "It could happen," she whispered. "Hello, Peter," she said, opening the screen door with a flourish. She stood up even straighter than usual, as though good posture alone might compensate for her red face, runny nose, and blackened eyes.

"Good *heavens*," Dilly's father said, seeing her. He took hold of Libby's shoulders, and Dilly thought for one amazing moment that he was going to sweep the woman into an embrace. "What in the world has been going on in here?" he asked Libby.

Libby pulled away from him and looked helplessly toward the two girls, as if begging them to come up with an explanation.

Dilly and Sasha looked at each other's tear-streaked faces, then looked at Libby—and then the three of them burst out laughing once more. "It's hard to say, Daddy," Dilly finally gasped. "I guess—I guess it's kind of a girl thing."

"Yeah. We're girly-girls, all right," Sasha said. "We love to cry—just for the fun of it, mostly."

"Would you care to sit down?" Libby asked, gesturing, as if Peter Howell had arrived for a dinner party. She kicked some soggy wadded-up tissues out of the way and gestured elegantly toward the sofa.

Sasha tugged at the hem of her T-shirt, which seemed to be all that she was wearing. Fortunately, it was huge on her.

"Good heavens," Peter Howell said again, still gaping at Libby. "Are you all right, Lib? What happened?"

Well, see," Sasha said, "there was this mean lady at the library, and she—"

"That's enough, Sasha," Libby said, trying to sound as though she meant business.

Her father shook his head, amazed, and his mouth twitched in what looked to Dilly like the beginnings of a smile. "I'd better not sit down," he said, obviously deciding to ignore his daughter's bizarre behavior, Sasha's skimpy attire, and Libby's apparent black eyes. "I ordered a big pizza from Nuccio's, and the guy said he'd be here in another ten minutes."

"Yummy. Pizza," Dilly said, trying to sound normal. But then she looked at Sasha and Libby and started to crack up again.

"*Yummy,*" Sasha repeated, laughing as if this were the punchline to a joke that only she, Dilly, and Libby could possibly understand.

"Sasha, shhh," Libby said, simultaneously patting Dilly on the back and trying to wipe away her own tears of laughter. "You're scaring Dilly's father, honey."

"Oh, I don't know," Peter Howell objected mildly, grinning wider now. "I'm pretty tough. And I definitely want to invite you two to join us for dinner. It looks like everyone could use some nourishment! But you're all going to have to pull yourselves together if you want to be able to choke down your share of the pizza."

Surprised by the thought, Dilly thought that her father looked surer of himself—and more *in focus*, in some odd way—than he had in years.

Sasha stifled one last giggle, and Libby flashed a glance at Dilly as if asking her whether or not she really wanted company for dinner. Or would she rather be alone with her dad?

Dilly hesitated only a second, then she gave Libby an almost invisible nod. "Please come," she whispered. "I want you to."

"All right, I will," Libby said, deciding on the spot. "*We* will, I mean."

"That's settled, then," Dilly's dad said, satisfied. "I'm heading back home in case Nuccio's is actually on time, for once."

"We'll be there in a couple of minutes," Dilly told her dad. "Sasha needs to get dressed—and I want to help Libby straighten things up a little."

"That's my girl," her father said approvingly. "See you three ladies at home."

Chapter Twenty-Two  A Beautiful World

"Don't sit *there*," Sasha told Dilly, moments after they'd boarded the southbound Ethan Allen Express. "Not unless you want to be facing backwards all the way to Penn Station."

"I don't," Dilly said, more excited by the train journey ahead than she was irritated at her friend's bossy and somewhat superior tone. She settled into a different worn seat and then peeked out of the window. Having kissed them both good-bye, her father and Libby were already starting to walk back across the empty tracks to Saratoga Spring's Amtrak station, which by now was nearly empty.

Dark clouds were rapidly filling the afternoon sky, as if in a movie in which the picture had been speeded up. Distant trees tossed restlessly, awaiting the coming storm. A moment later, comically big raindrops began to patter down onto the train and the surrounding concrete, polka-dotting every surface with dark circles.

Dilly saw both Libby and her dad duck their heads, as if that might somehow keep them dry. They hastened their steps and disappeared through a swinging door.

"Maybe we should have hired a chaperone for them," Sasha said, rolling her eyes. "I'm kidding!" she added quickly, seeing the look on Dilly's face.

"They're just sharing a ride, *Sasha*," Dilly said, trying to sound disinterested. "It would be dumb for us to have driven down to Saratoga in two cars."

Sasha nodded, a solemn expression on her face. "Dumb," she echoed.

"Oh, shut up," Dilly told her—but she *still* wasn't irritated. The prospect of visiting Sasha's family in the city was too thrilling for her to let Sasha's lame jokes get on her nerves. She had never been to New York City before, and Brooklyn was another mystery to her, as was Brooklyn Heights.

Two whole weeks! After that, Dilly would return to the farm alone, and a week later, Sasha would come up for Dilly's birthday celebration.

This new schedule was entirely their own invention, although Peter Howell, Libby Thorne, and Sasha's parents had all agreed that it was worth trying out.

"Tell me again about Brooklyn Heights," Dilly said as the train began to move.

She sounded a little nervous, and Sasha took pity on her and stopped teasing. "You'll love it," she replied. "Montague Terrace is actually kind of pretty, I guess, and it's just around the corner from Montague Street. *Obviously.*" The Thornes' big apartment was on Montague Terrace, Dilly knew. "And we can hang out on the Promenade," Sasha continued, "and look at the Statue of Liberty with all the tourists, if you want. And take Tater to the dog park, of course."

Tater was the Thornes' little dog, a shaggy white mixed-breed they'd adopted from an animal shelter in Queens a few years earlier.

"Are there skyscrapers all around?" Dilly asked, feeling a little shy.

"In the Heights?" Sasha asked, incredulous.

"Well, *I* don't know," Dilly exclaimed, defending herself.

"Okay, okay—calm down," Sasha said as the train picked up speed. "No, Brooklyn Heights is more like a village, re-ally—only it's a great big village in the city. There are lots of trees there, and most of the buildings are only a few stories high. But don't worry, my little country mouse," she added playfully. "Skyscrapers are only a subway ride away. Or we can walk over the Brooklyn Bridge to the city and look at them. That's fun, too."

Dilly—who did not like being referred to as a "country mouse," although she'd decided to let it pass, *for now*—thought for a moment. "Okay, maybe this is a dumb ques-tion," she finally said. "But isn't that kind of dangerous, walking across the bridge? I mean, won't there be a lot of cars whizzing by?"

Sasha shook her head indulgently. "There's a walkway for pedestrians," she said, sounding maddeningly patient.

Dilly stifled a sigh and stared out at the raindrops streaming sideways on the smeared window. She wished for a moment that she could magically transport Sasha to Southern California, where she, Sasha, would be the newcomer: the pale, overdressed, uptight, city mouse newcomer. Sasha would look like a vampire in Southern California, Dilly told herself. A short, cute vampire, true. But kind of weird and out of place, nonetheless.

"You'll like my friends," Sasha said, as if trying to think of a way to cheer Dilly up. "The ones who are still hanging around the city this summer, anyway."

"I guess you mean your 'real' friends," Dilly said, unable to resist the gibe.

Sasha shook her head, seemingly disgusted. "You're just *like* an elephant, aren't you?" she said. "Just like in that drawing you made! You never forget a single thing, Dilly. Give it a rest, already."

"Okay, okay. I'm giving it a rest. But the thing is, will your friends like *me*?" Dilly didn't like asking the question, but the thought of having to share Sasha with kids she didn't know was making her feel kind of funny— somewhere in the vicinity of her belly button.

"Well, sure they will," Sasha reassured her. "After the initiation rite, anyway. You're not afraid of rats, are you?"

"*Rats?*" Dilly squawked, causing a middle-aged woman sitting nearby to put down her magazine abruptly and begin searching the floor beneath her feet.

Sasha was gasping with helpless laughter. "I'm kidding," she finally managed to say. "About the initiation *and* the rats."

"Huh," Dilly grumbled, hiding her own relieved smile by turning her head toward the window once more. The gray sky was beginning to brighten, she saw; the Hudson was to the right of the southbound train now, and its rain-pocked surface flashed with the promise of sunlight.

"My mom's going to meet us at the station," Sasha said, trying to mend fences, as Dilly's father sometimes put it. "She says we can all take a cab home, instead of the subway. Because of all our stuff," she elaborated, kicking at the duffel bag crammed under her seat.

Dilly had never ridden in a taxicab *or* the subway, although she certainly wasn't going to tell Sasha that. "Whatever," she said. She thought for a moment. "What's your mother like, Sasha? Is she really as strict as you're always saying?"

"I don't know," Sasha replied, her voice soft. "I mean, don't tell her I said this, or anything, but she's really not so bad. At least I—" Sasha stopped suddenly.

At least I have a mom.

It was as though the words had been said aloud, but strangely, even the truth behind those unspoken words didn't make Dilly feel sad anymore. Rather, it was as though she were hearing a different sentence entirely: *At least I had a mom.*

"I'm sorry, Dilly," Sasha whispered. "I didn't mean to say that, or even to think it. It's just that I guess I appreciate my mom a little more than I used to. Not that I'm about to tell *her* that."

It was as though the Snob Hill papers were still working their magic—with Sasha, too, Dilly thought, amazed.

"And if you tell anyone I said I appreciate my mother, I'll have to hurt you," Sasha finished, glowering.

Dilly drew her fingers in a line across her closed lips and turned an invisible key at the corner of her mouth—exactly as she'd done when she and Sasha were eight years old.

The feeling wouldn't last—for either of them, she suspected. Sasha would go back to her old complaining ways, and she, Dilly, would find herself feeling cheated, clueless, and alone.

But what else was new?

"Look," Sasha said, pointing. "I think the sun is coming out."

Two gulls flying low over the river were illuminated suddenly by a shaft of sunlight. It was as if they were outlined in neon, Dilly thought, entranced. But they wouldn't look nearly as bright as they did if it weren't for the inky darkness of the river, or the dull soggy trees mounded on the water's far side, or the cloud-heavy sky.

"A beautiful world," Dilly said aloud.

It was just a little something she'd learned from her mother.

Epilogue  Heading Home

August 20

Dear Sasha,

Well, my dad and I are in the air again, flying home. Or flying back to Los Angeles and Pasadena, at least. Because I guess I can't say where home is anymore. Maybe my home is on Snob Hill!

Stranger things have happened.

I feel like maybe I do belong in Lake Luzerne, though—more than I ever did before. Anyway, we'll keep on coming every year, until I make my mind up for sure. But we'll come because we want to, not because we're trapped.

And hey, I wouldn't want to miss seeing your goofy face each summer! Assuming you want to keep on coming up to Lake Luzerne too, that is. It's a free country!

My dad just reminded me to thank you again for the birthday present. I do love New York, just like the T-shirt you gave me says! But they ought to make a T-shirt just for Brooklyn, too, because I like Brooklyn

even more. That was the BEST VACATION I EVER
HAD, even when your mom yelled at us for dyeing
Tater's ears with food color that time. But he looked re-
ally good.

I am *so* glad you and Libby are coming out to
California this Christmas!!! It is a *great* place for vegetarians.

We are gonna have SO MUCH FUN. We can go
Christmas caroling at the beach together, and put up a
plywood Santa on our front lawn, in between the palm
trees, and make ornaments, and wear cute matching
holiday outfits. And when we get tired of that, we can
go hiking (if we watch out for snakes) and surfing (if
we watch out for killer waves) with Frecka and Bean.

I mean Bucky and Flan.

I MEAN BECKA AND FRAN. (Oh, great, you've got
me doing it!)

Just kidding about the snakes, by the way. And the
matching holiday outfits. (And everything else I said!
HAHAHAHAHAHA!!!)

I *guess* I'm glad Libby is coming too. I really like
her, and I hate to say this, but I think my dad misses
her already. But grown-ups sure are weird. Watching
my father and Libby trying to get together is like waiting for two icebergs to bump into each other in the
middle of the Atlantic Ocean. I mean, you know it's
possible for it to happen, but you don't hold your
breath.

*Which I guess gives me plenty of time to get used
to the idea.*

*But at least my dad seems to <u>care</u> about some-
thing now. It's like he's waking up—a little, anyway.*

*Let me know if Libby officially breaks up with
Jean Paul Hottie, by the way. Because then I can officially start worrying. I look forward to becoming an
obsessive nut about something again!*

"Why <u>me</u>? Why <u>me</u>? Why <u>me</u>?"

*Oh, I forgot to tell you—we went down to the
cemetery yesterday, to say good-bye to my mother for
another year. I've done this six or seven times now, but
yesterday seemed different. My dad said, "Rest in
peace, darling," before we walked away, which he's
never done before.*

*But that wasn't the only weird thing. In a funny way,
I was sadder to leave my mom this time than I ever
was before. I mean, I feel closer to her than I used to,
but she also seems farther away. In fact, she seems
<u>gone</u>.*

It's a mystery.

*I put a flower from my mother's bouquet on old
Benjamin Thorne's grave for you, by the way. You know,
that Revolutionary War guy who was given Thorne Hill
in the first place? Anyway, I know how sentimental you
are about your ancestors (!!!) , so I did it for you. And
for him, just to say thanks for taking such good care of
the place for so long.*

Well, I'm going to say good-bye for now, Sasha, because my revolting little airplane meal is about to arrive. Hamster lasagna, curly brown salad, and papier-mâché pudding with a glowing red cherry on top is my guess.

Say hi to your mother and father for me, and LOVE TO BLUE-EARED LITTLE TATER.

Your friend in the new century, whatever it may bring!

Dilly

p.s. I'll e-mail you when I get home, but save this letter, okay? Because somebody in one of our families might want to read it some day. . . .

Sally Warner lives in Southern California, but she spends part of each year in the Adirondacks, where this book takes place. She is the author of many acclaimed books for young readers.

For more information about Ms. Warner and her books, visit her website: www.Sallywarner.com.